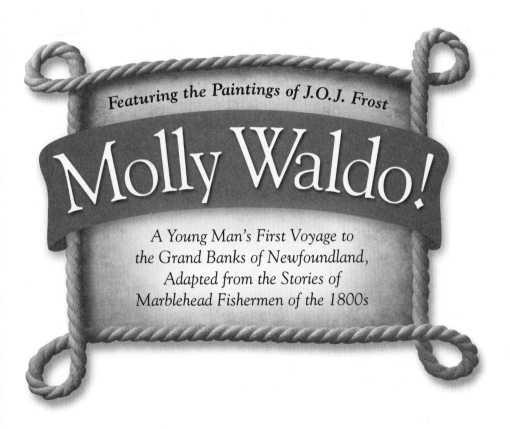

Featuring the Paintings of J.O.J. Frost

Molly Waldo!

A Young Man's First Voyage to
the Grand Banks of Newfoundland,
Adapted from the Stories of
Marblehead Fishermen of the 1800s

❅ **Priscilla L. Moulton and Bethe Lee Moulton** ❅

Foreword by PAM PETERSON
Director of the Marblehead Museum and Historical Society

The **GLIDE** *Press*
Boca Raton, FL

Molly Waldo!

A Young Man's First Voyage to the Grand Banks of Newfoundland,
Adapted from the Stories of Marblehead Fishermen of the 1800s

Published by

The **GLIDE** *Press*
2234 North Federal Highway, #438
Boca Raton, FL 33431
www.theglidepress.com

Molly Waldo! is a work of fiction. Names, characters, places, and incidents are the product of the authors' imaginations or are used fictitiously. Any resemblance to actual events, locales, or persons, living or dead, is coincidental.

All photos are courtesy of the Marblehead Museum and Historical Society, Marblehead, MA. Except for the map and photograph of Mr. Frost, images are paintings by J.O.J. Frost. Jacket photo is *A Bird's Eye View in 1867*. Grateful acknowledgment is made for permission to use these images and conduct extensive research in the Marblehead Museum and Historical Society archives.

Book Design: Peri Poloni-Gabriel, Knockout Design, www.knockoutbooks.com
Editorial and Production Support: Brookes Nohlgren, Books by Brookes, www.booksbybrookes.com

Publisher's Cataloguing-in-Publication Data

Moulton, Priscilla L.
    Molly Waldo ! A young man's first voyage to the Grand Banks of Newfoundland, adapted from the stories of Marblehead fishermen of the 1800s / Priscilla L. Moulton and Bethe Lee Moulton ; foreword by Pam Peterson, Director of the Marblehead Museum and Historical Society ; featuring the paintings of J.O.J. Frost.
    p. cm.
    ISBN 978-0-9836365-0-2
    Includes bibliographical references.

1. Grand Banks of Newfoundland — History — Fiction. 2. Fishing ports — Massachusetts — Marblehead — History — 19th century — Fiction. 3. Atlantic cod fisheries — Grand Banks of Newfoundland — History — Fiction. I. Moulton, Bethe Lee. II. Peterson, Pam Matthias. III. Frost, John Orne Johnson. IV. Title.

PS3613.O854 M68 2013
813.6 —dc23   2013944691

First Edition: October 2013

10 9 8 7 6 5 4 3 2 1

Printed in the United States of America

❧ For the Town of Marblehead ❧

IN HONOR OF

Lloyd Jackson ("Jack") Moulton
husband, father, sailor

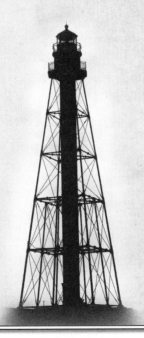

❧ *Table of Contents* ❧

J.O.J. Frost with Carved and Painted Cod

❋ Foreword ❋

J.O.J. FROST AND HIS PAINTINGS were the inspiration for *Molly Waldo!*, and his art illustrates the story perfectly. Frost's background is a Marblehead story in itself: his life reflects the changes that transformed Marblehead and the world at large in the late 19ᵗʰ century. Frost would have enjoyed this adventure, so like his own, of a young man aboard a fishing schooner bound for the Grand Banks. He would have been pleased and proud of the use of his paintings to help tell the tale because Frost was, first and foremost, a storyteller.

John Orne Johnson Frost was born in Marblehead in 1852. He grew up on Front Street, in a house near the harbor and public wharf. In Frost's boyhood, the landing was the center of activity for fishermen, both active and retired. Children gravitated there as well; as they played and fished, they listened to endless yarns. The men talked about fishing on the Grand Banks and recalled Marblehead's glorious days during the American Revolution and the heroic sea battles during the War of 1812. All the stories were filled with the pride that the old-timers felt for their town.

J.O.J. Frost went to sea at the age of 16, making his first voyage on the fishing schooner *Josephine*, bound for the Grand Banks. All went well and he signed on again, the second time aboard the *Oceana*. In May of 1869, the vessel was suddenly engulfed in a freak snowstorm. Visibility was at zero. With freezing conditions, the crew took turns to man the helm in 15-minute shifts. Like all the schooners at that time, the ship was powered by wind and had no instruments, except for a compass and a sextant. The crew knew they were off course, but had no way to get their bearings without a horizon line to orient them. All hands feared the worst. They thought they were doomed. Then, just as suddenly as it had started, the storm disappeared and the Oceana was able to determine her position and continue her voyage.

When Frost reached home safely, Amy Anna ("Annie") Lillibridge became his sweetheart. Of her he wrote, "She was then in her fourteenth year … she became my compass to steer by, and we never parted after our marriage until her death in 1919." Frost never went to sea again. Instead, he and Annie both went to work in her father's restaurant. Frost eventually opened a restaurant of his own and ran a bakery. During his lifetime, he held a variety of jobs: working as a cook, a carpenter, and occasionally writing for the local newspaper.

Meanwhile, Annie had planted a few fields with flowers beside their home on Pond Street. This was unusual at the time, because most land was used for edible crops. One day a lady came by from the Neck. (A cow pasture during Frost's youth, the Neck had become an enclave of fashionable vacation "cottages.") The summer resident saw the colorful flower bouquets that Annie sometimes put out by the roadside. The lady was delighted; she wanted as many as her carriage would hold, to decorate tables for a luncheon party she was giving the next day. Annie obliged. When the lady asked the price, Annie said she could have them at no cost. The lady insisted on paying, saying that she could give Annie a lot of business because her neighbors on the Neck would follow her lead. She was right; Annie Frost's sweet peas became all the rage. Annie's business became so successful that she was featured as an entrepreneur in a 1918 edition of McCall's Magazine—The Queen of Fashion. Frost helped sell her flowers from a wheelbarrow that he trundled down to Market Square on summer days.

It was after Annie's death that Frost began his final career. He missed his wife and was lonely. He had all sorts of tales to tell and no one to listen. He also had a deep love for Marblehead and wanted to ensure that the history of the town was remembered.

In 1922, at the age of 70, J.O.J. Frost began to paint. He said of himself, "Never painted a picture until I was past 70 years young." Why Frost chose painting as his medium is unknown. He could have written stories or songs or poems about the town. But, like Grandma Moses, he turned to paint to express himself.

Frost had never been trained as an artist. He used materials he had on hand—house paint, wall board, and odds and ends of wood scraps—to create his works. He had no understanding of perspective, no knowledge of anatomy, and no particular skill at drawing. When images failed him, he wrote at odd angles all over the paintings, usually in white paint and often with misspellings. What some might consider as artistic failings make his paintings charming and unique.

Frost did have talent in his ability to compose a scene and record events. His subject matter was Marblehead history, starting with the founding of the town and working his way through the proud moments of the Civil War. He considered himself a historian rather than an artist.

By the time Frost started painting in 1922, the town of his boyhood was not just disappearing—it was gone. The Marblehead of his paintings is a small fishing town of the post–Civil War 1860s and '70s: the harbor filled with fishing schooners; chickens, cows, and pigs in most of the yards; every house with a kitchen garden of vegetables. Oxen pulled heavy loads of wood and iron anchors; horse and buggies or stage coaches were the only transportation. By 1922, Marblehead Harbor was filled with pleasure yachts; restaurants and grocery stores were abundant; cars and trucks had taken over the roads. Frost painted the town of Marblehead as he remembered it from his youth.

More than 50 years after he had been to sea, Frost recreated scenes of fishing on the Grand Banks. He remembered everything from his two voyages as well as the endless stories he had heard from fisherman at the town landing. Frost painted the vessel *Oceana* lost in the snowstorm. He painted sea birds and fish and whales at play. He painted a true account of a man washed over-board and of ropes thrown out in a vain attempt to rescue him.

He worked tirelessly on his paintings, carvings, and ship models. He often put his work in an open wheelbarrow and walked down to Market Square, trying to sell the paintings for 25 or 50 cents. He didn't have much luck. He was friendly with the local photographer, Fred Litchman, who owned a photo studio on Washington Street. Frost would bring a newly completed work down to Litchman's, and Fred would make a picture of the new painting, usually with Frost in the photo. (One of those pictures precedes this Foreword of *Molly Waldo!*) Fred also displayed Frost's most recent creations in the studio window. Many people would come to see Frost's latest effort, but not to admire it. They would laugh and make fun of his work, scornful that it didn't look like "real" art. This seemed to have almost no effect on Frost; he went on painting anyway.

Eventually, beside his house at 11 Pond Street, Frost constructed a small building, which he called his museum. It was covered with his paintings, inside and out. It also held a collection of his carvings and a variety of other things he had collected over the years: a piece of wood from "Old Ironsides," ropes and anchors attributed to other ships, and his beloved "musical rocks." It cost 25 cents to go to the museum, and the proceeds were donated to the Marblehead Female Humane Society. The Female Humane Society still exists, but it wasn't sustained by large donations from Frost's museum! Visitors were rare. Almost everyone who came to his museum was from "away." Frank C. Damon, a newspaperman at the *Salem Evening News,* discovered Frost and wrote articles about him and his art. Frost sold very few paintings.

Even harder to sell were the "musical rocks." These remain a mystery. Frost claimed that some Indians gave him the stones. The rocks were stacked in formation and it seems that each had a different tone when struck. Frost was crazy about the rocks and loved to play them for visitors to his museum. He was quite put out when his listeners couldn't recognize the tunes he played. Was he bad at playing the rocks or were they less musical than he thought? The answer will never be known. At Frost's death, the musical rocks were arranged around his tombstone at Waterside Cemetery; they have since disappeared.

J.O.J. Frost produced over 200 paintings and carvings by the time he died in 1928. He left the bulk of his collection to the Marblehead Historical Society. For a long time, the paintings were largely ignored. However, after the Second World War, there was a surge of national pride. American folk art became popular, sought after, and valuable. Frost's paintings are now recognized as fabulous. Still left in Marblehead are some old-timers who remember that they could have had one for 50 cents! When Frost's home on Pond Street was sold, his art was uncovered on several walls during remodeling. It took a court case to resolve who owned the paintings. They were deemed part of the house and the property of the new owners.

J.O.J. Frost would be proud and happy to know how much his work is admired today. His paintings and carvings have their own permanent exhibit space in the J.O.J. Frost Folk Art Gallery at the Marblehead Museum and Historical Society. Adults and children from around the world come to visit and grow to love this artist and his work. We are delighted that those who cannot visit the Gallery can be carried into Frost's world by reading *Molly Waldo!*

PAM PETERSON
Director of the Marblehead Museum and Historical Society, Marblehead, Massachusetts
July 2013

Molly Waldo!

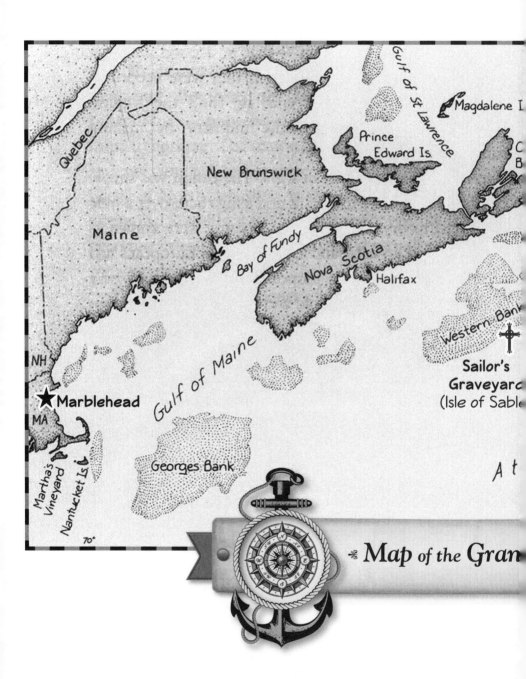

Quebec

Gulf of St Lawrence

Magdalene I.

New Brunswick

Prince
Edward Is.

C.
B.

Maine

Bay of Fundy

Nova Scotia

Halifax

Western Bank

NH

Gulf of Maine

Sailor's
Graveyard
(Isle of Sable

★ Marblehead

MA

Martha's Vineyard

Nantucket Is.

Georges Bank

A t

70°

Map of the Gran

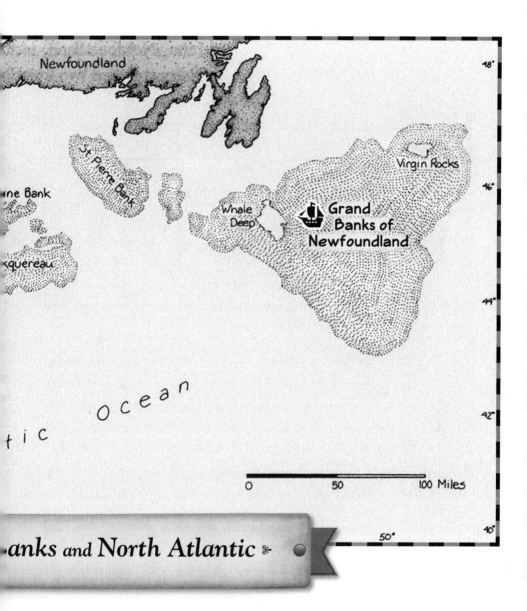

Newfoundland

St. Pierre Bank

ne Bank

Virgin Rocks

Whale
Deep

Grand
Banks of
Newfoundland

quéreau

Ocean

tic

0   50   100 Miles

anks and North Atlantic ❋

48°

46°

44°

42°

40°

50°

Who's Who in Molly Waldo!

I N **MOLLY WALDO!**, the characters and their relationships are fictitious. However, their experiences mirror those of real fishermen whose voices have been captured and preserved to the extent possible throughout this story.

Jon Bowen and **Tom Barton (Bart)** represent the young men who sailed from Marblehead, Massachusetts, to the Grand Banks of Newfoundland in the 1800s. Much of Jon's story comes directly from a biographical account: "J.O.J. Frost: The Life of a Unique Character in a Unique Town (lovingly typed by his granddaughter Ethel N. Frost)."

Captain Jeremiah Perry is inspired by the men responsible for the fishing schooners and for finding the fish. For example, Captain Thomas J. Peach, a Marblehead skipper, sailed to the Banks for 50 years, making 85 voyages. His memories are recorded in *History and Traditions of Marblehead* by Samuel Roads, Jr. Another skipper was Captain Edward B. ("Neighbor") Thompson, who wrote letters to his wife from the Grand Banks. Years later, portions of the letters appeared in newspaper clippings compiled by Frost in his scrapbooks.

Amos and **Old Orne** represent experienced Marblehead fishermen who taught younger men as they shared the watch, the dory, and the confines of a small schooner. Some of their knowledge comes from Captain Charles H. Snellen, whose stories were captured by Frank C. Damon in the *Salem Evening News*.

Stumper, the shoemaker, embodies the men who were disabled at sea from accidents and frostbite. In the winter, shoemaking was a source of income for the fishermen. Shoe shacks around town were social centers for swapping news and telling tales. The rooster story, recounted by Stumper, is extracted almost verbatim from Captain Snellen's "How the Gerry Engine Company's Gilt Rooster Went to Sea." It can be found in one of Frost's scrapbooks.

The **Fides** is a fictitious ship inspired by the *Josephine*, the schooner of Frost's first voyage, from August to October 1868. The other ship names come from historical records, though the events portrayed are fictitious.

The **September Gale** was conjured up from Frost's memories, as well as from an interview with a survivor of the Great Gale of 1846, Captain John Proctor. That interview was originally published in 1890 in the *Boston Sunday Globe*.

"Molly Waldo" was the joyful greeting exchanged when vessels from Marblehead met on the Grand Banks. Townsmen climbed into their dories to see familiar faces and swap yarns and messages from home. *Molly Waldo!* revives those voices from decades ago. So, step into your dory and come hear their tales.

*I had spent the hot summer's day carting split cod to the racks
around town where the fish dried in the sun.*

CHAPTER 1

❦ Signing On ❦

(August 1868)

I FIRST WENT TO SEA BECAUSE a rogue wave washed Elliott Walsh clean off the deck of the *Fides*. My friend was on night watch, when he was swallowed by the dark sea, just one day from home. That left Captain Perry in need of another hand on his schooner. At 16, I was the right age. There was just one way to earn a living in Marblehead … fishing … and I wanted more than anything to sail for the Grand Banks.

Perry knew me well; I'd been hanging around the docks since I could walk. I was small for my age, but pretty good at hauling … seaweed to the farms, timbers around the boatyard, and fish to the flakes. Hoping he would pick me for the vacant berth, I had spent the hot summer's day carting split cod to the racks around town where the fish dried in the sun. With just one more cartload to finish the job, I was tired. The day was over and I'd not seen the captain.

My empty wheelbarrow rumbled over the wooden wharf. Only after I had dropped it with a discouraged thud did I hear the booming voice. "Bowen, do you want to ship with me?" I pulled up to my full five-foot-two. My mouth went dry.

Turning, I looked up into a weather-worn face with intense hazel eyes beneath bushy brows. His salt-and-pepper beard seemed attached by a ring of dark hair that ran around the back of his head. Perry's bald crown shone like the sou'wester he wore at sea. "I've an open berth for a hard worker."

"Captain Perry, sir," I stammered. My head jerked; it did that if I was nervous. "I'll go if you'll take me, sir." My working since dawn had paid off.

"If the sharesmen agree, I'll give you $35, oilskins, and boots." Most captains didn't give their men any say about their shipmates. Captain Perry was different. "I want no quarrels on my vessel," he said. "Come back in the morning." Then, he strode away.

Meanwhile, Amos, the youngest sharesman, had pitched the last splits into my barrow. He was a huge man who kept to himself and wasn't one for chitchat. "That'll do it," was his signal that the loading was done. A twinkle in his dark eyes was the only hint that he might vote for me as a crewmate. Anxious to show my worth, I swung the barrow around and almost tipped the top-heavy load into the harbor. Amos smiled at my clumsiness.

Recovering my balance, I headed off the wharf with the cart. "Don't forget your heads," mumbled Old Orne as I passed. The oldest member of the *Fides* crew had survived the Gale of '46. Scarred forearms stuck out from his shirtsleeves that were cut off at the elbows. Leathery from years in the elements, Orne was tough, rugged, and clung to his ways. With no family of his own, he always collected the huge cod heads that the fishermen threw away and gave them to my ma.

"I'll be right back," I shouted. I kept the barrow rolling until I was around the corner, out of sight of the wharf. There, I slowed to a crawl. *How will I tell Ma?*

She was against my signing on. For two years, I'd had offers to ship. In April, when the fleet had sailed for spring fishing, my mother had refused my going. Of course I knew why. The sea had made her an orphan and a widow. On Sabbath, we would always climb to Burial Hill. My two grandfathers were listed on the obelisk in memory of the Great Gale that took 11 vessels and many of the town's men. From the monument, we would walk to my father's grave. He survived the Banks but not the Union Navy. In winter, Mother brushed the snow off the stone with a gloved hand; in summer, she traced Pa's name with bare fingers. As we would walk home, she always eyed the weathervane atop the church, a golden cod—the fish by which the town lived and died.

Laying the splits in neat rows on the flakes, I pondered how to break the news. Last spring, I'd tried logic: "Odd jobs don't pay much. I can earn more as a fisherman. On the *Black Hawk*, Wilbur gets ..."

Ma had cut me off. "Your brother keeps the roof over our heads. We don't need two roofs." I stayed behind to satisfy Ma. But this time, I had to go ... even against Ma's will. I was plenty old enough; some boys went at 14, some at 12. Staying home would make me a sissy.

When the barrow was empty, I had no more excuse for stalling. I rolled it back to the wharf where Old Orne was waiting. With hands as bent as hooks, he raised two buckets overflowing with fish heads. "For your ma's muddled cod," he said, passing me the pails. "There's nothing like it aboard the *Fides*." He winked; perhaps I had already been approved by the crew.

I thanked Orne, took the heads and walked toward the shingled house on Front Street, where I lived with my mother, brother, and three sisters. We would welcome a change from the cornmeal mush that we ate most days. The heavy wooden door scraped the floor as I shouldered it open. Ma was sweeping and bustled over. A once-white apron kept her cotton dress clean. Her brown hair was out of the way in a tight bun. Crows' feet spread away from sad eyes. I set the cod heads on the hearth. Happy to see the fish, Ma handed me an empty pail. "Jon, fetch me some water." I took the bucket. By going to the town pump, I could put off spoiling her good mood.

She went back to her sweeping and I started toward the door. With my back to her, I stopped. "Ma, Captain Perry asked me to ship with him." The broom became still. In the silence, I could hear my heart pounding away.

I swallowed hard. With a jerk of my head, I turned to face her and blurted out, "I'm going."

Her head dropped, heavy on her neck. She clasped the broom handle with both hands, as if it could give her strength. There was a long pause. My heart beat hard.

"So, Perry asked you, did he?" I nodded that he had. "Men. You're all the same." She shook her head slowly. "You don't know the heartache of us who wait. How could Jeremiah Perry sign my youngest son?"

"Ma, I'm no child. He asked me man-to-man and I accepted."

"Jon. You mustn't go. Look what became of Elliott Walsh." A tear formed in one of her eyes. "He was such a nice boy and so smart." Being a school-teacher, Ma knew every kid in town. The Walsh children were among her best pupils. "Such a waste. Such a waste." The tear fell and her shoulders shook. "Elliott survived that treacherous place to be washed overboard just one day from home. I can't let you fill his place." My coaxing got me nowhere. She started to weep. I felt sad and could not deny the fate of the neighbors she went on to name—the schooner of Robert Crowley sunk by a steamer, the dory of Joshua Jones vanished in the fog, and an endless list of men taken by furious gales.

Hearing her now confirmed what I already knew—that Ma would never grant her permission. My heart sank to think that I would have to sail without her blessing. But, I was determined. Lest I lose my resolve, I reached for the doorknob with the water pail in hand. I yanked the door open and bumped into my brother coming up the steps. Will's ship, the *Black Hawk*, was one of the many schooners currently in the harbor between trips to the Banks. No doubt he'd heard rumors about Perry's offer on the wharf.

"Why the long face?" he asked.

"She's against it," I said.

My big brother nodded with no hint about where he stood. "Go back in the house." Reluctantly, I turned to face Ma again. As soon as Will was through the door, she started telling him what I had done. "He thinks he can do as he pleases," she complained. "This boy is just plain ornery."

"He's getting too big for his britches." Will agreed with our mother, but winked at me. Like every Bowen before him, Wilbur had the sea in his blood and had been drawn to the Banks. Besides which, he was practical when it came to earning a living. "You'd best let him go, Ma. Captain Perry is one of the best. Under his command, Jon will learn a thing or two." I held my tongue, lest I ruin everything. "Before long, he'll get over it and won't go anymore." Will gently took the broom from her and stood calmly in its place. "Jon's a man now." It was almost too soft to hear. "You can't hold him."

Ma choked back her tears. "I suppose it's got to be. This day had to come." Whispering, she placed her hands on his upper arms and spoke to his chest. "It must be ever thus." She looked up into the face of her firstborn. "Month after month, I watch and wait and worry. When a vessel's coming 'round Point O' the Neck, I rush to the wharf and hope it's the *Black Hawk*." She looked over at me. "I guess with Jon on the *Fides*, I'll have twice the chance that the schooner coming will bring one of my sons home." With that, she picked up a cod's head and started cooking.

That evening, after supper was cleared, Ma handed me a worn duffle. "Here, Jon." In it were socks, mittens, nippers, and a cap. Without my knowing, Ma had been knitting. Despite the steamy August night, I donned the cap and nippers. The rugged woolen rings fit around my palms perfectly; they would protect my hands from cuts and rope burns while leaving my fingers free for baiting hooks. Ma had done all a mother could do to protect her son on his first voyage to the Banks.

The next morning, I was on the wharf early. The *Black Hawk* lay at the dock, preparing to set sail. The grocer's boy wheeled up barrels of pork, beef, and flour and left them alongside. Soon, he would return with packages of rice, tea, and chocolate. Will was loading on firewood for the *Hawk's* cookstove. I grabbed a cart and went to and fro between the vessel and Appleton's woodpile. It was the only way I could think of to thank him for convincing Ma.

Before long, Captain Perry strode onto the wharf with the ship's papers. I proudly signed "J. Bowen." He handed me enormous sea boots. Playfully, I slipped them on and clumped about. "They're big so you can kick them off if you go overboard." The skipper thrust oilskins at me. The waterproof slicker with its heavy, metal buckles was stiff and smelled of mildew. The sou'wester hat had a broad brim in the back to let the rain pour off in rough weather. On that bright sunny morning, I could hardly imagine needing them, but was proud to have my own oilskins.

"Be here before dawn tomorrow," the captain said. "We'll sail to Boston to get salt and be back by sundown." Hearing that, the younger boys on the wharf set up a regular din.

"Lemme go! Can I?"

"Enoch went last time. It's my turn!"

"Look at my muscle. See! I'll be good help loadin'."

Captain Perry told them only the crew would go. I threw back my shoulders and stretched tall. *Only the crew. That means me!*

"Go on up Washington Street to get your advance." Perry sent me to one of the men who owned the *Fides*. I got $15 to outfit myself; $20 was due when I came home from the Banks in three months.

At Dalton's Provisions I bought rugged flannel shirts and tough pants. Like the boots, they seemed way too big. "Don't worry, son," Mr. Dalton assured me. "By the time you come home, you'll be busting the seams." I hoped he was right. Next, I bought a fishing jacket, blue in color and lined in red; it was just like Will's, except mine smelled of new wool, his of fish.

"Spittin' image of his father and grandfather before him," I heard Mrs. Dalton say to her husband as I left the shop. I was taller already!

Shoe shacks were tucked into yards all around Marblehead.
We kids went there to hear wonderful, frightening tales of ice mountains,
ghost ships, sea monsters, whirlwinds, and screaming witches.

CHAPTER 2

❧ *The Gilt Rooster* ❧

BURSTING TO SHARE MY NEWS, I went down to Ferry Lane to see Stumper. Long ago, he'd been a fisherman who'd never missed a fare in 27 years. They said he knew the road to the Banks so well that he could get there without a compass, just by feeling the ship's gait. Then, in a September gale, a coil of rope caught around his leg. Since then, he'd poked along on a peg and gone to sea only in his mind. Stumper sat all day at his cobbler's bench and talked about the Banks.

Shoe shacks were tucked into yards all around Marblehead. When snow fell, the town's fishermen added to their meager earnings by stitching shoe soles to uppers. Stumper sewed shoes year-round. Folks gathered in his shop to debate politics. We kids went there to hear wonderful, frightening tales of ice mountains, ghost ships, sea monsters, whirlwinds, and screaming witches.

As I approached, the crystal ball in Stumper's window sparkled in the late day's light. When I was little, I'd asked him about the shiny sphere on its string. "See how it swirls?" he'd said. "That confuses 'em. The witches don't know which way to go. Keeps 'em away." Maybe a witch ball on Stumper's ship would have saved his leg.

A rusty anchor propped the shop door open. Stumper straddled the low bench, which had a curved seat on one end and a flat workspace on the other. A beam of sunlight reflected off his polished stump, almost as bright as the witch ball. Awls and knives were tucked into the holes around the back of the bench, within easy reach. Bent over his work and half deaf, Stumper didn't hear me coming.

"Ahoy, Skipper!" I stepped over the threshold into a cramped hut, 12 feet square. My shadow darkened his workbench as a pungent mix of leather, wax, and tobacco filled my nostrils.

"What's up, Young Bowen?" Stumper pulled a thread tight before looking up. When I didn't respond, he peered over his wire-rimmed glasses. "There's just one reason ya'd be sporting a seaman's jacket in this heat." A toothless smile opened above his long, white beard. How many of his stories had begun, "Someday, when ya go to sea …"? That day had finally come.

"I've signed on the *Fides* … with Captain Perry." His wrinkles deepened with pleasure. "So ya have, have ya?" He put down his work. "Jeremiah Perry will make ya a fisherman. And the *Fides* … she'll teach ya a thing or two. *Fides*. Did you know that's Latin?" I shook my head. He looked me over, head to toe. "Ya look just like your grandpa. I recall a time when we were cut-tails …" His voice drifted off, taking him somewhere else.

"Did ya ever hear how the Gerry Engine Company's gilt rooster went to sea? Seein' as how you'll be goin' to sea yourself in a few days, I'll tell ya 'bout a trick I put over on 'em once."

Stumper's tales were never two alike. He shaped his stories with the same care that he worked the shoes. Hunched over his bench, he would skive, scrape, and smooth the leather to make each pair unique. Same way with his stories. You never knew which pieces he'd pull from his memory and how he would stitch them together. I knew his yarns by heart, but never tired of his telling them, so I settled on a stool to listen.

I had shipped on the old Aladdin under Skipper John Widger.
The night before we sailed, I was skylarkin' about town with your
grandfather and our friend Dick. They could think of lots of things to
do, but they were not so handy in doin' them as I seemed to be. I guess
I could shin any kind of pole or mast and didn't need iron spikes for
footholds or shrouds with ratlines.

We were on our way home when your grandpa pointed to the gilded
rooster that served as a weathervane, perched on top of the flagpole in
front of the old Gerry engine house. "Ben, I'll bet you can't take that
bird down."

"Bet I can," said I. I pulled off my shoes and coat and in a very few
moments, I was at the top of the pole. I found the rooster was bolted on.
It swung on a spindle and I had quite a time in turnin' the nut. I wished
many times afterward that I had left it there. But, I went through with the
game and brought it down safely to the other boys.

"You take it," said I to your grandpa. "You're the one that wanted it."

"No, you brought it down. Keep it."

Then I turned to Dick and asked him if he didn't want it.

"No, sir," he said, very decidedly.

I suppose I should have climbed the pole and put the rooster back in
place, although it would not have been as easy as the first time. It takes
both wind and muscle to drag yourself up 50 to 75 feet, with nothin' but a
smooth pole to cling to and that growin' smaller every foot you rise.

It was close to midnight. Not a soul was on the streets. Nobody had
seen me do the stunt. So, I took the bird home with me and hid it in my
sea chest that was goin' aboard the Aladdin the next mornin'.

But I couldn't go to sleep. I knew they'd miss the bird in the mornin'
and they'd be right down after me. So, I got up and took the rooster down
to the woodshed and hid it under the wood. Father heard me and made
some sort of remark, which I didn't catch and didn't try to. I got back
into bed and pulled the covers over my head so I could not hear him.

But, then I began to think the woodshed would be the first place they'd begin to search. I'm goin' to take him aboard the vessel, I said to myself.

I stole out quietly, went down to the wharf, unfastened my dory, and rowed out to the Aladdin. I placed the rooster between the blankets in my bunk. But, when I came back, father's sharp ears caught my footsteps on the creaky stairs. "What the devil are you doin' up all night?" he asked.

"I've been sick."

"Are you alright now?"

"Yes, sir."

"Well, get back into bed and call me if you need anything."

I didn't sleep much. Before I was up, Nat Bliss, the chief of police, knocked at the door and told my father about the disappearance of the rooster and wanted to ask me about it. "That boy don't know a damned thing about it, Nat. He's been home all night, sick."

That seemed to satisfy the chief for the time bein', and to cut the story short, Dick and I went aboard the Aladdin and we put to sea that day. The rooster rested in my bunk all that summer. When about 60 miles off the coast on the return trip, I took it out.

"Dick," I said. "I've kept this bird long enough. It's your turn to take care of him now."

"Not on your life!"

"To hell I pitch it then," said I. And with that, overboard it went. I felt kind of sorry, because it was just as bright and shiny as the day I took it down. I'd kept it wrapped in an old flannel shirt. It had not been exposed to the salt sea air.

My step proved to be a wise one. No sooner had the Aladdin anchored in the harbor than who should pull alongside in a dory but Nat Bliss. "I got a warrant to search your vessel," he said to Captain Widger.

"The hell you have! What for?" asked the skipper.

"For the gilded rooster weathervane that young Benjamin took from the Gerry firehouse flagpole the night before you sailed." So, they had nailed me with the trick.

"I don't have your old rooster," said I. "Come aboard and search all you damned like." But Captain Widger and Uncle Mose Proctor would have none of it. They hustled Nat back into his dory, told him to pull ashore and mind his own business.

I heard afterward that Nat reported back to the engine house something like this: "You fellows got me into a hell of a mess. Why, I thought Uncle Mose Proctor would throw me overboard. That boy hasn't got your rooster."

True, wasn't it? I guess he's restin' about where I dropped him, decades ago.

Stumper paused and turned philosophical. "It bothers me still to think about it. I don't suppose I was any worse than any other boy, but there's a good deal under the surface of any fellow that doesn't quite square with the moral code. I don't know how you're ever goin' to stop it until human beings are made without human nature … and ya know when that can be expected to happen."

With a lot of unfolding of his bent self, the old seaman got up. "Take a lesson from this leg," he said, stumping toward me. "If ya can't tell the truth about it, best not do it." He put out his hand to shake mine. His grip was sticky with wax, but I didn't mind. In my 16 years, he'd never offered his hand. "Jon, I wish your grandpa could see ya. Which vessel is it again?"

"The *Fides*," I reminded him.

"Ah, yes, the *Fides* … she'll teach ya a thing or two. *Fides*. Did you know that's Latin … Stands for all kinds of things … like bein' honest, bein' upright, bein' a man men trust … the *Fides* … a good choice for your first voyage."

A lump rose in my throat, so I turned to go. "I'll come to see you before setting sail," I promised. With that, I left him in the doorway, with summer sunlight glinting off his white beard, his wooden leg, and the witch ball.

"We sail day after tomorrow. With a little luck,
we'll be first home with a fare to spread over every flake in town!"

CHAPTER 3

❧ *Readying the Fides* ❧

THE NEXT MORNING, I WAS on the wharf before the sun was up. Through the gray of dawn, happy whistling announced Tom Barton. Bart swaggered toward me; a wad of tobacco puffed out his scarred jaw. Then, he spit into the harbor with perfect aim. Bart had a bad reputation in town but a good one at sea.

Like most kids in Marblehead, Bart had grown up without a father. However, he couldn't claim a dad lost to fishing or the War with the South. Bart was born out of wedlock to Sally Barton and he was shunned for it. A troublemaker in school, he'd dropped out early, earned a little money, and poured it all into liquor. "Stay clear of that Tom Barton," Ma had warned my sisters and me. No one had wanted him on their vessel, but Jeremiah Perry had been short-handed after the war. He signed Bart at 15 and somehow turned the daredevil into an able hand. After four years on the *Fides*, Tom Barton was known to be fearless in a storm and able to fill his dory with fish as fast as the next man. Some said he'd be a sharesman before long.

Bart was all muscle and twice my bulk. As he approached, I extended my hand and felt my head jerk. A yellow bruise rippled beneath Bart's blond stubble. I willed my hand to steady; his jaw relaxed. Abruptly, Bart grabbed my hand with a numbing grip. Just when I thought my eyes would water, he released me. "See ya aboard … Bowen Boy." He took pleasure in blowing the Bs in my face. He headed for his dory, leaving no doubt about who was low man on the totem.

With easy strokes, Bart rowed toward the *Fides*, anchored in the middle of the harbor. I was wondering how I would get out there, when Amos arrived on the dock. "Come with me," he said.

It being low tide, I followed him down the steep incline to the float where many rowboats were tied. To reach his dory, we had to climb across two others. With long legs, Amos straddled the high sides without any fuss; I scooted after him using my arms to get over the gunwales. I hoped no one was watching. Finally in his boat, I plopped onto the stern seat. Amos pushed us through the maze of other boats and took up the oars. With big, muscular arms, he rowed as easy as I walked. Never looking over his shoulder, he just knew where he was pointed. The boat that would soon be home was closer with each stroke. From bow to stern, the high sides had a graceful sheer. The black hull had a blunt bow and a square stern. I liked the saucy tilt of the long bowsprit and the bright-green stripe at the waterline. "She looks mighty fine," I said.

"She's old but seaworthy," Amos replied. The *Fides* had two masts and was about 60 feet long. "Captain Perry knows her whims and can make the old girl get up and go," Amos said with his next stroke. Living in a seaport, I'd grown up where men used "she" and "her" to refer to boats. To hear Amos, you'd think the *Fides* was as much a woman as my ma.

We came alongside and I clambered aboard. "Want to see the cabin?" Amos asked. "The captain and sharesmen sleep here," he explained as I scrambled down the ladder into a dim space below the deck. I saw a wood-burning stove and two berths on each side, one above the other. A big locker ran around the edge. The lids served as seats with stowage below. "That's the platform," Amos explained. "If you're ever sitting there, it's because you're in a heap of trouble with the captain or waiting for a fierce storm to pass." It seemed Amos was a lot more talkative with water under him.

"That's my berth," he pointed to one on top. "Want to see yours?"

We climbed back up on deck and then down another ladder into a stench of mildew and sweat. This was the forecastle (but everyone just said "fo'c's'le"). I would live here with the other hired hands—George and Bart.

"You'll sleep there." Ducking under the low ceiling, Amos pointed to the upper bunk on the starboard side. An empty box, about five feet long, was above another strewn with dirty socks, shirts, and rumpled bedding. The ship's hull was the outer wall; a board on the inner side would keep me from falling out. The beams supporting the deck were just three feet above the bed. Being small would come in handy for once. Ma had sewn me a bed tick; the canvas bag stuffed with straw would soften the wooden box. "That's where I slept as a cut-tail. The growl of the anchor chain will be your lullaby." I couldn't imagine how Amos had squeezed his bulk into that tight space, but knowing the space had been his eased my thoughts of its more recent occupant, my friend Elliott.

Going straight up through the forecastle was the foremast, a huge timber mounted on the keel. A table was built around it, with leaves that folded down out of the way. "Meals and heat will come from here. See how it's gimbaled?" Amos rocked the cookstove on special supports that kept the burners horizontal. Around the top was a railing to keep the pots and kettles from tumbling onto the floor when the *Fides* heeled over in the wind or pitched about on high seas. The fo'c's'le walls were grimy from smoldering wood fires and pipe smoke. Had Ma been there, she would have set to scrubbing.

"Come on. It's time to raise sail."

Amos led me back up to the bustling deck. At the wheel, Captain Perry gave no orders. The men just knew what to do. On the windlass, the Dawson brothers were raising the anchor. Like my pa, Charlie and George had answered Abraham Lincoln's call to save the Union; unlike Pa, they'd returned home to fish. They moved in unison, were dressed alike, and had the same sideburns, mustache, and beard. *Don't ask me who is who*, I thought.

At the foremast, Bart raised the foresail. Watching the ease with which he moved, I understood why all the girls had a crush on him. Strong and nimble, he could run up the ratlines faster than anyone in town. Despite Ma's warnings, I hoped we'd become friends.

That left the main halyard for Amos and me. Hoping my schoolmates were watching, I hauled on a rope that pulled the big sail up the aft mast. As the main went up, Old Orne took hold of the mainsheet, a rope that fed through several blocks to control the position of the sail as it filled with wind.

Before I knew it, we were sailing out of the harbor. Not yet loaded with provisions, the *Fides* was light. We fairly flew over the water. My spirits soared.

Old Orne joined me on the foredeck. "Have ya ever fished, Bowen?"

"Aye. From the rocks around the harbor."

"That ain't fishin'."

"I guess not, sir."

"Save 'sir' for the captain. 'Orne' will do."

"Aye, s—Orne."

"Well then, I reckon ya need to know a thing or two about salt."

"I reckon so, s—Orne."

"As ya might expect, dead fish rot in no time … stink, too … unless ya pack 'em in salt. So, we dress the fish as soon as we catch 'em. We split 'em open and take out the guts. Then, down the chute they go, to be sorted and salted and stored in the hold." With no teeth, Orne actually said, "'orted and 'alted and 'tored," but I got his drift. "Too much or too little salt can make the whole lot worthless. But, if ya get it right, they'll keep for months."

"Who does the salting?"

"On the *Fides*? Me." A crooked thumb pointed to his chest. "Under the watchful eye of the skipper, of course." He tipped a respectful head toward the man at the wheel. "He'll decide when our salt is wet."

Being a Marbleheader, I knew that would be when the hold was loaded to the brim. "And then we'll sail for home with a full fare!" I raised my arms in triumph.

"Boy, ya sure remind me of your grandpa. It's too many years since I shipped with a Bowen. Welcome aboard."

"It's a privilege, sir … I mean, Orne."

Next thing I knew, we were entering Boston Harbor. The other crew-members lowered sails, watched for rocks and shoals, and prepared to tie up. We were soon alongside a huge wharf with enough pilings to build a whole town. Little was said during the entire operation. *How do they know what to do when?* I wondered. *How long will it be before my tasks are second nature?*

Wanting to do my share, I put my all into loading the heavy barrels of salt. I was hot and sweaty, but I didn't mind one bit. Without salt, the *Fides* and her crew were good for nothing.

With the job done, we were preparing to cast off when Bart hollered, "Hey, look at that!" We all gaped as a man pedaled down the dock perched atop a two-wheeled contraption.

"What is it?" I asked.

"Not sure," admitted Bart, "but I want one."

I couldn't imagine balancing on such a thing, but the man rolled along as easy as could be.

"You won't catch me on one of those things," Charlie said.

"What will they think of next?" Captain Perry mumbled. The man circled round the wharf and rode away. "Now I've seen everything," the captain said.

On our way back to Marblehead, Bart went on and on about buying a riding machine. I didn't think a fisherman could ever earn enough to buy one. Just the same, telling my friends I had seen one would make them envious.

Wind from the southeast and a calm sea gave us a smooth ride home. A huge sail billowed out in front of the *Fides* and pulled us over the waves. "Come out on the 'sprit!" Bart challenged. With nothing but whitewater below, he walked on the long pole that stuck way out from the bow. Bart didn't have to stretch out his arms to keep his balance; at the tip of the bowsprit, he scooched around a cable that held the forward edge of the jib, the luff. He grinned back at me and insisted, "Come on!"

Full of jitters, I straddled the beam like a horse. I faced forward to watch the oncoming swells. Gripping tight with my thighs and my hands, I went out about a foot. The bowsprit rose and fell as the *Fides* cut through the waves. A rhythmic swoosh filled my ears; salt spray was sharp on my lips.

"Enjoy the ride," Bart shouted. "It don't get better than this." My dangling legs brushed against some ropes. I pointed and threw a quizzical look toward Bart. "We stand on those to douse and furl the jib."

Bart said "we." That meant that sooner or later, I would have to help to lower and tie up the big sail. I couldn't quite imagine standing on those flimsy lines. Seems Bart read my mind. "Just wait 'til you're out here in the dark, trying to douse the jib in a storm. Ya'll be hugging the widowmaker and praying for your life." *Calling the bowsprit names seems like asking for trouble*, I thought. Just then, the billowing canvas snapped in the fresh breeze, as if it agreed.

BACK FROM BOSTON WITH 150 hogshead of salt, we spent the next day putting aboard the other provisions. Mackerel bait in 10 precious barrels, 2½ cords of firewood, 25 pounds of candles, barrels of pork and beef, bushels of potatoes, 8 pounds of tea, 20 pounds of rice, and 15 pounds of chocolate. The galley was stocked with hardbread, sugar, and molasses. On the deck, we nested the dories and stowed the hooks and lines.

Getting ready to catch 20,000 fish was hard work! My arms ached. My back ached. Bart teased, "Don't work so hard. Ya'll get no extra pay!"

When the *Fides* was ready, Captain Perry announced, "We sail day after tomorrow. With a little luck, we'll be first home with a fare to spread over every flake in town!" The best price was paid for early fares, so more than spirited rivalry was at stake in being the first back with a good catch. Perry pulled me aside. "I've watched you, Bowen. You're not big, but you stick hard at a job. That's worth as much as a bundle of brawn. Make the most of tomorrow's holiday. You'll need the remembering of it in days to come."

As I walked up Front Street, I heard a girl's voice calling, "Jon. Jon." It was Dorothy Bartlett. Her brother Emmett, my best friend, had shipped out in April on the *Caroline Jane* and had not come home yet. Every day, Dorothy watched through her rooftop scuttle for her brother's return.

I approached. Dorothy stood in her doorway with a large package. "Here … for your duffle." She thrust the bag at me. "I used Black Joe's recipe with lots of rum and molasses."

To hide the jerk of my head, I turned a little as I opened the sack. Out poured the sweet, spicy smell of Joe Froggers. The cookies were huge, the size of the lily pads near Joe's Tavern.

"Thanks," I mumbled.

"I always bake them for Emmett."

Dorothy sounded a little sad, so I tried to cheer her. "As soon as I sail with these cookies, your brother is sure to come home and say I pinched them." Dorothy smiled.

"If that will bring him, I'll go and bake you another batch," she teased and disappeared into the house.

"Thanks," I called after her; it didn't nearly express how pleased I was. I got to wondering if there was something new about the way Dorothy tied her hair. She looked different and kind of pretty. The spicy aroma wafted up from the bag. I was tempted, but resisted. I would save the Froggers. No matter how long the voyage, they would stay soft and delicious at sea.

The next day, I put my duffle and bedding aboard and went to say goodbye to Stumper. The witch ball twinkled as I came up Ferry Lane; the door to his shop was propped open. His glasses were down on his nose as he tapped a sole with his little hammer.

"Ahoy, Skipper!" I hailed him.

This time, he was waiting for me. "What's up, Young Bowen?" I told him about going to Boston and seeing the bicycle and riding the bowsprit and even about the Joe Froggers. When I finally ran out of steam, he said, "So, you're becoming a real storyteller, just like your old friend Stumper." We both laughed.

"I'll never tell yarns as good as yours."

"Well, just wait 'til ya've been to sea. Speaking of which … I never went past Half Way Rock without tossing a copper for the gilt rooster." He reached down, opened the little drawer under his bench, and pulled out a small cloth bag. He gently undid the faded yellow tie and poured out three coins. "These are lucky ones," he said, handing me the coppers. "They've been here, just waiting for me to pick 'em up. When ya go by Half Way tomorrow, ya toss these: one for you … one for the gilt rooster … and one for me."

"I will. I promise." The coins made a solid clink as I put them back in the bag and retied the string. Then, I clasped Stumper's sticky hand in farewell.

As we rounded Point O' the Neck ...
I waved to Ma, even though she was just a speck 'midst the figures on shore.
The Fides shaped her course out into the Bay, leaving our families astern.

CHAPTER 4

❦ *Off for the Banks* ❦

EARLY ON AUGUST 10ᵀᴴ, we set out for the Banks. The weather was perfect. My sisters and Ma waved white handkerchiefs with the other women gathered on the docks. Townsmen came aboard the *Fides* to hoist the mainsail, then the foresail. Everyone sang "Shenandoah" as we cranked the windlass to raise the anchor.

With a lively crowd on deck, we sailed up and down the harbor, towing the orange dories of those who would stay behind. We came close by another schooner where the crew was washing out their fare. "Molly Waldo!" they shouted. "Molly Waldo!" we hollered back with gusto. Every ship in the harbor repeated the refrain as we sailed past.

"Ya shan't hear that cry for many days," said Old Orne. "Not 'til we meet a Marblehead vessel on the fishing grounds." I wondered how long it would be before I hailed a townsman on the Banks.

As we rounded Point O' the Neck, the home folks drew their boats alongside. Goodbyes were said. A final cheer went up. I waved to Ma, even though she was just a speck 'midst the figures on shore. The *Fides* shaped her course out into the Bay, leaving our families astern.

With the lighthouse still in sight, Captain Perry steered close by Half Way so that we could throw our coppers. Hitting the jagged rock would bring good fortune. Bart hurled a coin and let out a whoop as it struck the granite. Ma would disapprove of tossing good money away, but I'd promised Stumper. I mustered my longest throw and sent my first copper flying. *One for me.* It struck. *Now, this one for the gilt rooster.* I took careful aim and the second penny hit. *And this one for Stumper.* Just as I released the third coin, the *Fides* picked up speed. The copper arced over the water and splashed into the sea, sending up a little geyser of spray.

Only Bart saw the splash. The rest of the crew had scattered to trim the sails. "Serves ya for showin' off," Bart scoffed. "Should have quit while ya was ahead, kid."

He had a point. Three coins were a fortune. I wanted to say, "I did it for Stumper," but Stumper wasn't to blame. I feared my miss would bring bad luck. I hoped the two hits would compensate for the coin that fell short.

"Off for the Banks now!" called the skipper. The *Fides* headed out on the broad ocean, pushed by a following breeze. As the hull rose and fell with the swells, so did my spirits. I wasn't sure what to feel—the thrill of being on my way or the scary truth of no turning back.

We were ploughing along at a steady speed, when Amos came up to me with a sandglass in his right hand and a rope with knots in his left. "This is the log line. I'll show you just what our gait is." He threw one end of the line into the water and let it run out through his hand. "When all the sand reaches the bottom bulb, stop the line and count the knots. That's the log." He showed me how. "Ten this time. You try it."

I gathered up the rope and tipped the sandglass over. The knots bumped rough against my palm as the line ran out. I grabbed tight just as the last grain of sand fell. "Now get your count," said the sharesman.

I hauled the rope in. "Ten!" The same count as Amos, on my first try. "Maybe it's beginner's luck. I'll do it over." Throwing the log line was fun.

"It never hurts to check twice." Amos chuckled and watched me practice.

"Ten!" I was getting the hang of it.

"Well, then, we must be going ten knots!" Amos teased. "Now we'll report that to the skipper. He figures our whereabouts and notes it in the logbook."

After soup for supper, we drew lots for the four-hour watches. Bart would stand watch with taciturn Charlie, who had not spoken since leaving the harbor. I drew the midnight watch with Amos. My lucky copper seemed to be working.

"Tumble in, but leave your oilskins on," advised Amos. "The wind's strong. It will save time if you're called up."

I crawled into my berth, but felt uncomfortable in my bulky slicker. Sounds of fitful breathing came from another berth. George wheezed. *How strange to sleep with a grown man just inches away.* I missed my warm bed back on Front Street, but squelched thoughts of home and pulled the scratchy wool blanket tight to my chin. Finally I dozed off, but soon footsteps pounding above my head woke me. A thunderclap made me feel trapped in the berth, so I climbed out and poked my head up the hatch. Lightning flashed all around us.

The jib was down and the mainsail was much smaller; some of its canvas was lashed to the boom. Dousing the jib and reefing the main had caused the commotion. No one had called me out; I guess they'd figured I'd be more hindrance than help. They would have been right.

I was terrified. *Will lightning strike us?* Remembering the coin that had splashed beside Half Way, I crawled back into my bunk and pulled the blanket over my head. It did not shut out the thunder that boomed around us.

My stomach felt bad and I couldn't sleep. Just before midnight, Amos fetched me. We replaced Charlie and Bart, who went below to sleep. The storm had blown past, but I felt peculiar. Big swells made the *Fides* pitch and roll. As the ship heaved, everything in my stomach pushed up to my throat. Amos guessed what was about to happen. "Get to the rail."

I started toward the high side. Amos grabbed my arm and turned me toward the leeward side. In the nick of time, I was on my knees, right next to the water. Everything inside of me emptied into the sea. I wished Ma was there to hold my head. I clung to the ship, feeling miserable and spent. I would have given anything to stop moving.

"Come take the helm," Amos said. I could barely rise, but I didn't want to disappoint my shipmate. I stumbled up and grasped one spoke of the wheel. "Look to windward," he said. "Watch the horizon, not the waves. You'll feel better." He was right.

In the rough seas, the *Fides* wanted to go every which way. Thank goodness, Amos stayed beside me and kept us on course. His steady hand did most of the work, but being at the helm got me through that miserable watch. At 4:00 A.M., with a hint of light in the east, I crawled into my berth and fell into a deep sleep.

WHEN I WOKE, THE SUN shone over the endless sea with no land in sight. I felt more myself; the seasickness had gone with the storm. At midday, Captain Perry got out his sextant, a black triangle with a shiny curved base and a special eyepiece. At exactly noon, he took a sight on the sun and measured the angle to the horizon. Next, he did some figures and marked our position on the chart. "It's not hard to navigate a vessel. If you can add two and two and take two from six, you can navigate. Just watch your compass, keep the log going, take the sun, and know how to figure." I was good with numbers in school, but somehow I didn't think it was quite as easy as the captain claimed.

That second day, the crew broke me in proper. They taught me their lingo and quizzed me on all the parts of the vessel. I hauled on the sheets and made things fast. I trimmed the sails and secured the lines on belaying pins and cleats. I'd never heard so many new words in one day; my brain was bursting.

The third afternoon got squally. I eyed the billowing jib. Someone would have to work on the bowsprit above the seething foam. As the sky darkened, Bart brushed past me. He placed one foot on the beam with whitewater crashing below. I forced myself forward. The bowsprit was plenty ominous.

Bart spun around and shouted, "Here's no place for a kid. Get away." I stumbled backward and steadied myself against the dories.

The captain shifted our course and the powerful sail made a terrible fuss. George took control of the flapping jib sheets. Amos was at the foremast, ready on the halyard. At the tip of the bowsprit, facing aft, Bart bounced about like crazy. He grabbed the luff. "Let her down," he hollered. Amos controlled the descent of the jib. Jouncing above whitewater, Bart tussled with the wild canvas, tamed it, and brought it down. Oblivious to the waves that would have washed me away, he lashed the sail down with the stops. In no time, the job was done and Bart was back on deck. George and Amos had moved aft to reef the main. With less canvas flying, the skipper fell back to our original course. All the strange words I had learned were pretty handy in a squall.

We put up with a good deal of thunder and lightning, rain and hail, but it didn't last long. When things calmed down, I said to Bart, "On the 'sprit, you were mighty fine."

"Dousing's tricky. Lose your balance and it's over." He didn't stay serious for long. "Aw, shucks, that one was easy … even ya could 'a done it." *Not me*, I thought. "I'd take ya out with me, but Perry don't want to lose another boy. Not yet anyway."

Bart was showing off, but he'd earned it. He'd downed the sail as easy as folding Ma's laundry. He'd worked on the plunging spar as calm as could be. "Maybe you'll teach me a thing or two," I said, and my head jerked.

"We'll see. Ya's not quite ready for the widowmaker."

In fact, every hand on the ship was needed. So, the next morning, I got my first lesson on the ratlines and the bowsprit. Bart made it look so easy. I was sure I would tumble into the Atlantic, but tried to hide my fear. I was a Bowen and would do what I must.

On the fifth evening, I could no longer resist the Joe Froggers in my duffle. After a supper of stewed beans, I shared one with Amos while we watched the sun sink into the ocean. "See how the sun is dropping into a bank that's heavier on the north than the south? That says the wind will bear southerly. If you see a shooting star tonight, watch its slant. If the slant is northwest, the wind will be northwest tomorrow." Amos was young, but he seemed to know more than men twice his age.

That night, we did see shooting stars. A clear night sky and the Milky Way made a majestic dome above the *Fides*. We both craned our necks to look up. "That's a sight reserved for mariners," Amos said with a gentle awe that I didn't expect from such a hulk of a man.

The next night, he said, "Look astern." An unwavering line marked our path through the waves. "What do you see?"

"Wake as straight as an arrow."

"That's your seaman's eye." I thought it praise, until he added, "Look again ... with your soul." I went to the rail. The ocean shimmered, as if the stars had thrown sprinkles around us. "What do you see?"

"Lights." It was beautiful. "Lots of tiny lights."

"God's smallest creatures are singing 'Halleluiah,'" he said in a hush.

I was mesmerized by the fluorescent wake. "Guess that's another sight reserved for mariners," I said.

"Aye."

I waited a while to build up my nerve. "Amos," I said, "you know a lot about lots of things." No comment. "But, back in town, no one would guess it."

"Probably not."

"I was thinking ... you're a real good teacher. Ma works at the school. You could, too ... that is, when you're not out fishing." My head jerked a little.

Amos looked at the compass, looked at the sails, but didn't look at me. We sailed on in silence for what seemed forever. *Maybe I've offended him.* "Amos, I'm sorry for butting in; it's none of my business."

"Now that's probably true," he spoke at last. "But you meant no harm." Silence fell again. After a long time, he asked, "How are you at keeping a secret?"

It made me think of Stumper; he'd said *fides* meant being upright, being a man men trust. "Never had to keep any, but think I'd do fine."

"I think so, too." Amos checked the compass and the sails. "Back in town, folks have their ideas about what makes a man: things like where he came from and whether he has a house. Out here, Nature is the judge. Out here, the measure of a man is in how he lives, not what he owns ... or whether he can read." He choked on the word *read* and his shoulders slumped. *Amos doesn't know his ABCs!*

Many men couldn't read. When boys started to fish, they stopped going to school. Ma was a stickler for book learning, so I knew my three Rs as well as my sisters did. But, I never let on, lest kids call me a sissy. Amos kept quiet because he couldn't read; I kept quiet because I could!

"Folks *do* have strange notions when it comes to judging others." I chose my words carefully. "But, knowing your letters comes in mighty handy, for reading charts and such." Amos didn't seem to notice my head jerk. I dared to go on. "Amos, I could show you a few things about it ... when we're on watch." That's when no one else would be around. "After all, you're showing me all sorts of things."

"I suppose I am, Bowen." His eyes looked wet, but maybe it was just a glistening from the night sky. He changed the subject. "What's our heading?"

I read the compass and checked the horizon. The sea was calm and there were no vessels in sight. With all well, I slipped below and brought up my Bible. Ma had made me bring it and now I had a reason to open it. I sounded out the letters, just like Ma had taught me.

During that watch, Amos learned to recite the alphabet and trace the shape of A and B with his finger on the deck. He would be reading in no time. To signal the end of the lesson, I tucked the Bible under my shirt. The earliest light of dawn was in the east. "Go look under the stern," Amos said. "Tell me what you see there."

I stepped aft, pressed my belly against the gunwale, and peered down toward the keel. "A small fish, all by itself," I reported to Amos at the wheel.

"That's the rudder fish. Now look under the bow."

I walked forward, leaned over the rail and spotted a small fish like a mackerel. I returned to the helmsman and said, "Another little fish, all by itself."

"That's a pilot fish. Those two will stay with us, all the way to the Banks."

"How come?"

"Guess it's just one of Neptune's gifts to the mariner."

Even when Amos couldn't explain something, his way of thinking about it was different from most men. I liked that.

"*Porpoise ahead!*" ... *As the* Fides *pitched down,*
Charlie hurled the harpoon straight into the back of a porpoise.

CHAPTER 5

❈ *Ganging the Hooks* ❈

N O ONE BUT THE CAPTAIN seemed to care about navigation, but I was fascinated by the log line, the sextant, the compass, and the chart. Captain Perry invited me to join him in the cabin while he did his figuring and wrote in the logbook. Each day, he noted something about the wind and sailing conditions, as well as our latitude and longitude. A typical entry looked like this:

August 13ᵗʰ. Commences with fine breezes from the south. At 6:00 P.M., blowing fresh from the west. Double reefed the sails. Middle part squally, rough sea. Latter part more moderate. Spoke the schooner Superior *of Salem bound for home with 12,000 fish. Latitude by observation 43.02, longitude 65.19. Boiled pork and potatoes for dinner.*

At noon on the sixth day, Captain Perry took a reading of the sun. "Let's go see where we are, Bowen." Below in the cabin, he spread out the chart. "Where does latitude of 43.22 and longitude of 62.22 put us?"

I studied the numbers on the edges of the map. I found 43° on the right side and 62° on the bottom. With my right index finger, I drew one line across horizontally. I imagined a vertical line coming up from the 62. "About here?" I pointed uncertainly where the lines crossed.

"Pretty close. Maybe you'll be a navigator by the end of this voyage." The skipper seemed pleased. "Take a close look. What's written there?"

I studied the lettering. "Isle of Sable."

"Right. That's what it says on the chart. But, every skipper knows it as the Sailor's Graveyard." He showed me our position southeast of Halifax. "This is no place to lose our bearings." He double-checked his calculations before he added, "We're halfway to the fishing grounds."

That day, we saw flying fish and a school of whales, just like the ones in Stumper's stories! Perry sent Bart aloft as a lookout. He scrambled up the ratlines on the foremast to the crosstree, the spot where a wooden bar crossed the mast. He would stand up there and sing, with the wind blowing back his blond hair. I hoped that someday I would be brave enough to be a mastheadman, high aloft, singing to the gods.

From up there, Bart could spy vessels—three so far, but none from Marblehead. Near the Graveyard, he shouted, "Porpoise ahead!" There was great excitement. Charlie grabbed a harpoon and climbed out in the stay braces that ran from the end of the bowsprit down to the waterline. Charlie was barely above the bow wave. As the *Fides* pitched down, he hurled the harpoon straight into the back of a porpoise.

"Hard up!" Charlie yelled. The captain brought the *Fides* into the wind. Bart, George, and Amos brought the jib down. The schooner pitched; the porpoise flew through the water, making it bloody as can be. Just when the harpoon line was running out, the porpoise weakened. We all took ahold of the line to pull him aboard. That was my first sight of a porpoise, close up, and a sorry sight it was.

Charlie and George skinned him and hung the meat in the rigging to dry. It looked like the beef from the cows in town. The fat from the jaw was carefully saved. Porpoise oil brought a fancy price from the jeweler, there being nothing better for clockworks. A few days later, George fried the meat like beefsteak. "Relish that taste," Amos advised. "From here on, you'll be eating fish, fish, and fish."

AFTER A WEEK AT SEA, I was accustomed to my bulky sea boots and oilskins. Maneuvering in the awkward gear was important. When things got rough, all hands tended the sails in blowing spray and pelting rain. Often high seas broke over the deck. I learned to do my share without stumbling too often.

I had my sea legs. I wasn't as agile as Bart, but I could move about the ship without lurching or grabbing on to something in a moderate sea. When it was rough, I still struggled to keep my balance above and below deck.

While I was becoming more secure on the *Fides*, I was starting to worry about how I would manage in a 15-foot dory. The rowboats were stacked on deck, running fore and aft between the two masts. Dories 1, 3, and 5 were on the port side; 2, 4, and 6 on starboard. Painted bright orange, they nested one inside the other, like spoons, with their flat bottoms on the deck and the top open to the rain and waves. To drain, the boats had a little hole in the stern; of course, a wooden plug would close up the hole to keep the dories afloat when we launched them. The top boat held the oars for the stack; the handles were worn smooth and the tips brightly painted. Rolled up beside the oars were simple sails, sewn from flour sacks; if the wind was right, those would carry the dory downwind with little effort.

One day, I came upon Old Orne running his crooked index finger over the big black number 5. "This one's lucky," he croaked in a secretive way. "Always caught more in this one." The dories all looked the same to me, but Orne thought different.

Despite no teeth and a limp, Orne had everyone's respect. Bart had told me, "If ya want to find fish, watch Orne. The old man has a knack. I wager he's half fish himself." In a few days, the crew would draw lots for the boats. I hoped Orne would draw Dory 5.

The old man didn't seem to mind foolish questions, so I asked a lot of them. "Why do we sail so far from home just to fish?" Going 150 miles to Newfoundland seemed like a peck of trouble.

"Well … guess it's 'cause fish like the place. The warm Gulf Stream and the cold Labrador Current meet up and stir up a banquet for all the sea creatures. And for us, the fishermen, God put a nice big shelf on the ocean floor, where we can set down our anchors and lines."

"So it's shallow?"

"Aye. The captain will sound the bottom. He'll throw a line with a lead to see how deep it is. Forty fathoms means we're on the edge."

"How much is a fathom?"

"About so." Orne stretched his arms out. Six feet, I figured.

"So 40 fathoms will mean we're there?"

"Depends what ya call 'there.' It's a country. You can sail 350 miles and still be on the Banks. We'll be there when we find the fish, not before."

That day, the *Fides* surged along under a fine breeze; there wasn't much to do. Orne leaned against the dories and lit his pipe. I leaned next to him and asked, "When was your first sea voyage?"

A throaty chuckle led to a cough, but finally Old Orne started his tale. "Fourteen I was when I went to sea, hardly loose from my mother's apron strings. It takes more than a week to learn the ropes, Bowen. I'm still learning things from the sea."

"How did you rate that first fare?"

"I went as the cook. Think of it," he laughed his growly laugh and coughed a bit. "A green boy of fourteen cooking for seven hearty seamen! The skipper soon decided I was better at the lines than the frying pan. I've always been lucky with fish. I caught fish big enough to haul me overboard. But it was cold. I went aloft one day and counted 22 islands of ice. The next morning a berg was only 300 feet from us. Looking over the side, I saw the prong. We didn't waste any time leaving that ice astern."

"Do you think I'll get to see an iceberg?" It sounded exciting.

"Ya better hope not. Moving fast in a current, an ice island can ram and sink a schooner. A dory doesn't stand a chance. We see more ice early in the year. This being a fall fare should spare us, but fog's another story. Of that, we'll see plenty. Cold and so thick you can't see the end of your dory. Even an old-timer like me fears he'll be swallowed and never see his vessel again."

Orne's talk of ice mountains and fog made me shiver, despite the sun overhead. Feeling a jerk in my neck, I changed the subject. "Is there anything besides cod and halibut?"

"Oh, sure. All sorts of fish and queer growing things will come up on the hooks. I've hauled up apples, peaches, and corn. They grow in the ocean, related to the land variety, but different, of course. Now and then, I've caught a ground shark; they're 25 feet long and rare to find near the surface. Back then, we sold their oil for rheumatism and bone troubles." He rubbed his clawed hands. "Could use some of it myself these days." A coughing fit put an end to our talking.

AS WE DREW CLOSE TO the fishing grounds, Amos said, "We need to ready the lines and gang the hooks." My shipmates were clustered near a heap of lines and wooden buckets. "We'll use the dories to set the trawls," Amos explained as he lifted a big coil of rope. "With two men in each dory, we'll lay these lines on the bottom with anchors; a buoy on each end will mark its location. What we need to do now is tie on the gangings and the hooks."

Amos showed me how to prepare a skate by tying branch lines, every six feet, along the ground line. At the end of each ganging, we tied a hook—50 hooks on each 50-fathom line. The skate was wound carefully into a wooden bucket. "This is the tricky part," Amos explained. "If the skate tangles, the line won't run out of the tub; you'll lose time and may have to cut your line."

Several skates were coiled into each bucket. Each dory would carry two or three tubs. I did my arithmetic; a typical dory had 1,200 hooks!

Tying the hooks on was tedious work. With his stiff hands, Old Orne was a bit slower than the others; that made it easier for me to copy what he did. I worked beside him.

"Don't see why they had to switch from handlining to trawling," he grumped.

"What's the difference?"

"When I was your age, we fished from the vessel. Lowered the lines right over the rail, pulled the catch on deck, and threw the fish into wooden pens—a box to hold the catch of each man. Of course, I was just a cut-tail. Kept track of the fish I caught by cutting the tail off. Got paid for each one. The system was fair and simple."

Orne stopped to cough and bait a couple more hooks. If I kept still, he'd tell me more. "Then someone figured we'd catch more if we spread out in dories, away from the mother ship. One man, one dory. Ya row out, anchor, and set a line over each side. In a good spot, the fish bite smart and soon ya've got all your dory can hold."

"I thought Amos said there would be two men in each dory." I was confused.

"That's for trawling. The French came up with this new way of fishing for a bigger catch." Orne sucked air in past his toothless gums in disgust. "When they first put out those long lines, we'd steal 'em. Marbleheaders called it unfair competition. Now we've joined in their madness."

"What's wrong with trawling?" I asked. As far as I could tell, Amos and the others had no quarrel with longlining.

"It's too complicated. You need a mate to set and haul all this gear." He waved at the lines and buoys. "One mate maneuvers the dory while the other pays out 50 fathoms of ground line. From end to end is a mile or more. That's a lot of line to set and to haul, without any snarls. Besides, it's easy to foul another trawl. If you have to cut your line, you lose all your gear and your catch." Orne shook his head and coughed for a while.

"Trawling is for the rich. They're building bigger, faster vessels to carry twice the men and take twice as many fish. That takes money. Big money. The little guy won't stand a chance. Those new vessels will get to market first with their big catch. They'll drive the price down. Mark my words. There'll be hell to pay."

He pushed aside one tub and started on another. He glanced about to see who was listening, and then whispered, "Perry's still got his doubts about trawls. Brought me along to out-fish 'em, and I will." He chuckled. "I'll give 'em a run for their money." We worked in silence for a while, ganging the very hooks that made him so upset.

After thinking about all he'd said, I countered, "But, Orne, even if you catch more fish than the others, that won't put an end to the trawls."

"You're right, son," he said sadly. "I'm a dying breed, just like this old girl." He squinted up the mast. "Next season, the skipper will command a new schooner that they're building across the Bay in Essex. She'll be long and fast and one profitable ship under Captain Jeremiah Perry."

To me, it sounded exciting. "Will you sign on?"

"Not me. I'm too old. The *Fides* is plenty fast for me. I've got no heart for trawling." He glanced over at his crewmates. "Don't misunderstand. I've no quarrel with a dorymate. Being alone in a pea-soup fog is unnerving. But, I'm old-fashioned," he croaked. "I want to be master of my dory ... master of my destiny."

After that, we ganged the hooks in silence. I wondered, *Which is better —handlining or longlining?*

"In the old days, when your dory was full, ya'd raise an oar in the air.
Then the others would know you're on a good spot
and would come to fish there."

CHAPTER 6

❊ Handlining with Old Orne ❊

O N AUGUST 21ˢᵀ we let down the jib and sounded. The report was "no bottom," so we sailed on for another 40 to 50 miles. Seeing about 15 vessels at anchor, we sounded again and found 40 fathoms!

To celebrate being on the Banks, I took a line, baited the hook, and threw it over. Something grabbed on hard. I had a halibut, the first fish of the trip! Bart ran to the bowsprit; they let the jib down. "Let 'im run a bit," Orne said. I did, but hung on tight to the line for fear of losing him. After a few minutes of watching, Orne said, "Now bring 'im in." I did, with a lot of help. Charlie brought the gaffstaff, a long stick with a big hook on the end. He and George gaffed the enormous fish aboard.

We set the jib again and sailed northward. The next day, we sounded 28 fathoms and found a hard bottom. "Down with the anchor!" cried the captain. For the first time in 12 days, we let the sails down and stopped surging forward.

With the anchor holding firm, we set up the pens and the splitting table. The fishing began. Through the night watch, we fished. My Bible stayed tucked in my berth. There was no reading lesson.

In the morning, we dressed the catch. Charlie (the throater) cut the throat of the fish, slit down the belly, and took out the livers. Next, Bart (the header) placed its neck against a square pin. Off came the head! On the other side of the table, Amos and George (the splitters) cut the headless fish in two with a single slice, and then cut out the sound bone, its backbone. The fish slid down a chute into the hold, where Orne (the salter) packed it away in salt. I hauled the salt for the packing.

As soon as the catch was salted down, the dories were lowered into the water. Amos and George jumped into Dory 1; Charlie and Bart into Dory 3. With long strokes, they were soon off in different directions, looking for the best spot to set their trawl. "Leave it to Captain Perry to put the Dawson brothers in competing boats," Orne chuckled. He was in a good mood, having drawn his lucky boat. He dropped down into Dory 5 with his handlines and rowed off.

That left me alone with the captain. I figured we'd launch a fourth boat. I was disappointed. While the others fished, he drilled me hard. With my eyes shut, I coiled and uncoiled lines until my hands were full of rope splinters. "Some dark night, it will serve you well," was all Perry said. I shimmied up the foremast as far as I could, which was about halfway. I scrambled up and down the ratlines. At noon, the captain brought out the sextant, took the sun, and made me figure our latitude.

The dories were just specks on the horizon when the captain started eyeing a distant, dark cloud. "That fog bank is headed our way. Ring the men in."

"Aye, sir!" I rushed to the bell and yanked hard on the lanyard.

"Keep ringing 'til every man's accounted for."

"Aye, sir!" I could no longer see the boat that had gone furthest away. Another loud chime told the dorymen where to find us. I felt mighty important and no longer questioned why Perry had kept me aboard.

A dory bumped alongside. Orne threw his painter up to the captain. Once tied up, he pitched his fish aboard—cod weighing 30 to 40 pounds each and one 60-pound halibut. Oblivious to the bouncing rowboat, the old man leapt aboard. By now, the fog was upon us. Orne peered out for the others. "Doesn't take long to retrieve a handline," was his only comment.

The fog was thick; I could barely see the length of the *Fides*. "One in. Two more to come." Captain Perry strode toward the dory tackle. "Keep ringing, Bowen."

For the next hour, I rang the bell and peered into the gray. At last, a fuzzy orange bow approached. I was relieved to see my watchmate. Having pulled just one trawl and left one to retrieve in the morning, Amos and George had a small catch. No sign of Bart and Charlie. My arm was getting sore, but I kept clanging. Finally, their dory came alongside. Having pulled both trawls, they had a decent catch—a bit of this and a bit of that. To my way of thinking, Orne had the best haul.

THE NEXT MORNING DAWNED CLEAR. A schooner with a bright-green stripe at her waterline came into view. "Bodgo!" sounded across the water. A vessel from Marblehead was hailing us.

"Molly Waldo!" replied the captain. It was the *Madison*, away from home since April. The Dawsons clambered into a dory to tell their friend, Joe Hinckley, that he had a new son. Much cheering rose up at the happy news. Then the *Madison* sailed on for her next berth. "They've already got 15,000 fish aboard!" George reported when they returned. "Joe will be holding his baby boy in no time."

"And holding his wife, too." Charlie sounded envious. The Dawsons didn't talk much, but that morning I knew they missed their families, just like I missed Ma.

Bart and Charlie headed out with fresh tubs; George and Amos went off to find the trawl they'd left in the fog. Orne came over to me. "Captain's agreed. I can take ya with me today." He winked. "Told him a Bowen can't start out setting trawl; first he needs to learn about real fishing."

I grinned as I jumped into Dory 5 after the old man. He pushed us away before the waves could crash us into the *Fides*. The dory rocked like crazy;

I stumbled toward the stern. "She's crank when empty," Orne said. "But, she's steady once she's loaded." Fearful of being seasick all over again, I hoped we'd be loaded soon. "Set yourself on the rower's seat." Orne moved to the stern, leaving the oars to me.

I pulled a long stroke. Then another and another. About a mile from the *Fides*, Orne said, "Throw the anchor over." I did. "Now, we'll put out a line on each side." Orne threw a line over the starboard side; I did the same on port. "When the sinker strikes bottom, pull it up a few feet. Cod are greedy. They swim along with their mouths open. They'll swallow anything. Put the hook where they'll find it."

As the dory pitched about, I tried to do what Orne did. "Wrap the line around your palm." He circled a line around his hand. I started to do the same. "Wait. Where are your nippers?"

"Back on the *Fides*. Aren't they for the cold?"

Orne dug into a wooden box and pulled out a spare pair. "Always hand-line with nippers." I put them on. "Alright. Wrap it." I wound the line on top of the nipper in my right hand. "When ya feel a bite, tug to set the hook. Otherwise, the fish will steal your bait. Timing's the secret."

We waited. Orne went on. "Every fish bites different. A halibut will tell ya when he's on your line. He runs and ya better let 'im if ya want to keep your gear. A cod hauls down hard." Just then, a fierce jerk would have sliced into my flesh, had my hands been bare. "That's a cod. Set the hook." I tugged. "Ya've got 'im!" Orne sounded pleased. "Haul 'im in. Cod don't fight." Hand-over-hand, I pulled in 150 feet of line with a heavy fish at the end.

At last, my prize came into sight. When I heaved the 30-pounder over the gunwale of the dory, its square tail grazed my cheek. The slippery body had three fins on the back and two on the belly. The upper body was golden with white below. But, there was no time to admire my catch.

"Bait up for the next one," Orne said. I pulled the hook from the cod's mouth and started to fish again. I baited the hook, set my line, and pretty soon had hauled in another cod. With the weight, the dory steadied.

"In the old days, when your dory was full, ya'd raise an oar in the air. Then the others would know you're on a good spot and would come to fish there." Orne was wistful. "No point in raising an oar these days. The trawl lines will just tangle."

The dory was low in the water. To me, it seemed full. The old man kept fishing. Suddenly, something powerful pulled on my line. "Ya've got a halibut." Orne was excited. "Let 'im run for a while." He felt big. I didn't want him to get away! "Now ... pull 'im in," Orne said.

Only after much hauling did the great fish come up. Before it could get its head down to run again, Orne struck it a numbing blow with a belaying pin. "Let's haul 'im over the rail." In sloshed the giant fish. The dory tipped and the gunwale was almost underwater. "Stay calm," said Orne. "Shift your weight." I leaned back and the boat leveled.

Now, our dory had all it could hold! I pulled up the anchor, took up the oars, and started the long row back to the *Fides*. The other dories were already there. Bart caught and secured my painter. "Will you look at the 80-pounder!" Even Bart was impressed.

The crew gaffed the big halibut aboard. Orne watched while I pitched the cod up by myself. When all the fish were on deck, he waited for a wave to lift the dory and leapt onto the *Fides* with the ease of a dancer. Trying to copy him, I stumbled over my big boots, but no one noticed. They were too busy counting the catch. Amos and George had the most fish; they'd pulled three trawls—the one left overnight plus two new ones. Bart and Charles were not far behind, having set two trawls. With the huge halibut, Dory 5 made a good showing. My lucky penny was still working.

I was tired and very hungry. I had eaten nothing since breakfast. However, there would be no supper until all the fish were salted away. Everyone took their places and the dressing began. After supper, I tumbled into bed—too tired to talk, too tired to think, too tired to teach Amos to read.

The next morning, knowing there would be no food until supper, I ate a big breakfast of fried halibut. That day and the days that followed,

I handlined with Old Orne in Dory 5. Sometimes rain set in and the fish bit like crazy. One hazy afternoon, the fish refused to bite.

"Think we should try another spot?" I asked.

"Fish can be funny." Orne made no move to haul in the lines or anchor. "One September, years ago, I was on the *Mary Dorothy*. She sprung a leak. Nothing to do but pump like hell and make for land, which we did. At St. John's, we got her fixed, but lost a lot of time. We were back on the Banks in mid-November; most of the vessels had gone home. We anchored and started fishing from the vessel, but not a fish could we raise. 'There's fish here, I'll take odds,' I said. 'Maybe it's a night school.' Some fish bite by day. Others bite only at night. Come dark, we went at it again. Hardly were the lines down before the fish began to take the bait and bit like fury 'til midnight. Half the crew went below; that left the other half. The fish came in better than ever. In ten nights, we took 10,000 cod off the grounds—beautiful fish, some of them running up to 50 and 60 pounds. It breezed up considerable, but we gave the vessel more cable to make her ride easy. The rougher it was, the better the fish took the bait." Suddenly, he seemed to remember I was there. "What was it ya asked, Bowen?"

"Just wondered about trying another spot," I reminded him.

"No. We'll wait right here for the sun to shine." A few minutes later, sun broke through the haze. Wouldn't you know, the cod took the hooks!

We had a full load and I moved forward to raise anchor. "I knew your grandpa ... your dad, too." Orne rarely spoke about men, just fish. I sat down. Orne pulled in the port line and coiled it. "They were both fine dorymen. I talked to Captain Perry. Tomorrow, you'll handline from Dory 6."

"Alone?!" I felt proud, but scared at the same time.

"You're ready ... and you're a Bowen. That reminds me ... this belongs to you."

Orne reached under his oilskins with a gnarled hand and pulled something shiny over his head. Nestled in his wrinkled palm was a dull brass pendant on a chain. It was a portable compass. "The needle has weathered many a season, but it reads as true as when I got it."

I was in awe. "How'd you come by it?" A beautiful little instrument like that might belong to a captain, but not a fisherman like Orne.

"Haul in the anchor and I'll tell ya." I was taking up the oars when he slipped the chain over my head. "To answer your question, we need to go back 20 years.

"Back in '46, dories were new. The old-timers didn't believe in 'em, but us youngsters went out: me from the *Samuel Knight*, your grandpa from the *Warrior*. The two schooners were berthed close together. Every day your grandpa and I bet on who'd catch more cod.

"One day, Jonathan said, 'Orne, if you out-fish me, I'll give you my compass.' I figured he was joking, but next day, he brings out this compass on its chain." Orne coughed for a bit.

"How did Grandpa come by a fancy compass?" According to Ma, the Bowens had always struggled to make ends meet. Grandpa wouldn't have had money to buy something so fine.

"Won it in a card game. From Ben."

"Ben. You mean Stumper?!"

"Aye. Before he lost his leg, he was Benjamin Boyle. It was a friendly game. Your grandpa didn't want his winnings. But, Ben said, 'Hell, Jonathan, you won it fair and square,' and made him take it." That sounded like Stumper, for sure.

"So," Orne went on, "each morning, the compass changed hands based on the catch the day before. More often than not, your grandpa had it, but on the morning of September 18th, he passed it to me. That day was one of the most beautiful I've ever seen on the Banks. The sun was shining clear in the sky, but away at the northward, there was a black bank of clouds, like a thunderstorm about to break. The tide was running strong and the lines would not touch bottom. They stood out straight.

"Seeing the storm coming, Captain Proctor called me back to the *Samuel Knight*. He sailed off the Banks to the westward, thinking to get away from the rest of the fleet and into deeper water. Later we saw four or five vessels, among 'em the *Warrior*, *Sabine*, and *Trio*, all of Marblehead." Orne's voice cracked and he set to coughing again. Once recovered, he finished. "Ya know too well the fate of those ships and their men. May Neptune guard their souls."

I'd been pulling long strokes and we were nearing the *Fides*. "That morning before the storm, I caught but a handful of fish." Orne paused a moment. "But your grandpa was low in the water with a boatload. I've had a debt with him ever since."

Two more strokes would bring us to the *Fides*. I slipped the compass under my shirt and buttoned up. We pitched our fish on deck, just like always. That evening, as I fetched the salt and ate supper, the metal was cool against my chest. Finally, alone in my bunk, I fingered the pendant under the blanket. Convex glass protected the compass rose. The face with north, south, east, and west had given Stumper and Grandpa and Old Orne their bearings. My thumb ran over the metal case. Something was etched on the back. I was dying of curiosity, but lighting the oil lamp would draw attention. I'd have to wait for daylight. I fell asleep holding the disk and dreamt about surprising Stumper when I got home.

The prospect of filling the dory with fish made it more than big enough.
However, bouncing alone over choppy whitecaps,
I was a small man in a tiny boat.

❧ *Becoming a Blooded Banker*

SEPTEMBER DAWNED WITH CLEAR WEATHER and choppy seas. On deck early, I pulled the compass from my shirt and looked at the fancy script: *Veritas Fides Honorque.* Stumper had told me that *fides* was Latin for "trustworthiness." Before I could puzzle out the rest, I heard footsteps behind me. I stuffed the treasure away beneath my shirt.

"Hey, doryman, time to launch your boat!" Bart shouted. We loaded Dory 6 with the anchor, oars, bait, and lines. As we lowered the boat, Bart scoffed. "You're wasting your time, kid. Handlines are a thing of the past." This was a special day and I wasn't going to let Bart ruin it. I jumped in and shoved off.

The prospect of filling the dory with fish made it more than big enough. However, bouncing alone over choppy whitecaps, I was a small man in a tiny boat. After rowing for 20 minutes, I was thirsty. I looked about for the bait-butt. Every dory carried a wooden box that held a leather water pouch, a foghorn, spare nippers, and a little hardtack. It was from a bait-butt that Orne had pulled the spare nippers on my first day of handlining.

Dismayed, I realized my mistake. In my hurry to get away from Bart, I had failed to bring a bait-butt. If I went back to get one, Perry might question whether I was ready to be a lone doryman. His keeping me aboard the *Fides* would be hard to bear. The sky was clear and I had Orne's compass. I decided to keep going without the emergency supplies.

I tossed over my anchor. Before setting the two lines, I pulled out the compass and took a bearing on the schooner. She lay due east; Orne's dory was due south. My empty dory pitched violently, so I was relieved when the first fish bit. Soon I was pulling in cod and baiting hooks, just as Orne had taught me. The dory steadied and got low in the water. I thought she had all she could hold when a halibut bit. This time I didn't have Orne to help, but I knew the drill.

First, I let him run. Next, with all my strength, I pulled the fish to the gunwale. I whacked it on the head a couple of times before it stopped fighting. It was over 100 pounds! With my mightiest heave, the halibut came up and brought most of the ocean with him. The rail was under and frigid water came in fast. *Shift your weight.* Orne's voice echoed in my head. As I took a new stance, I slipped and fell backward. But the dory righted itself. The halibut and I were inside, piled atop the rest of the fish.

Shaken, I lay still for a moment; Orne's compass was cold on my chest. I caught my breath and inched forward to pull up my anchor. Every wave threatened to swamp me. I wanted to throw a few fish back, but Orne would never do that. I set my feet firmly and took up the oars. The wind blew one way and the tide ran another, making a rough ride. Pulling my load through the chop was hard work. For sure, a shark was cruising alongside, waiting.

Inside me the feelings were as turbulent as the ocean outside. I was proud to have a bountiful catch for the vessel … but, would I make it back to her? One big wave could end my days as a doryman. Even if I made it, I had let Orne down. I had gone solo without a foghorn or water. Taking unnecessary risks was foolhardy.

With my back to the *Fides*, I pulled hard on the oars—again and again and again. My heart pounded. My chest was tight. I was angry with myself. Finally, I looked over my shoulder. *I'm closer than I thought! And there's Old*

Orne! Dory 5 was just ahead of me. Knowing Old Orne, I bet he'd never been too far away.

As I rowed the final yards to the *Fides,* my fear eased, as did my anger. Charlie and Bart gaffed the huge halibut aboard. At supper, everyone was in high spirits. I was a hero. One more fisherman meant fewer days 'til home. I forgot I was a lucky fool who didn't deserve their praise. Instead, I celebrated being a doryman by sharing a Joe Frogger with my shipmates.

THE NEXT DAY STARTED much the same. The trawlers went off in pairs. Orne rowed away in Dory 5. I set out in Dory 6, this time with my bait-butt. I found a good spot about a mile from the schooner. As I caught plenty, my dory sank lower and lower. Orne had warned me about being greedy. "One fish too many and you'll go straight to the bottom. A single wave can take you to a cold grave." Even so, I preferred the danger of too many fish to the shame of too few.

That day, I was so busy pulling in cod that I didn't notice the fog rolling in. The clammy air closed around me. I'd lost sight of the *Fides* and could not hear the clanging bell. Aboard the schooner, fog felt different. Its cold fingers had never made me shiver. My knees started to shake in the eerie silence; my heart started to pound. I yanked up my anchor and rowed to escape the gray.

After a few panicky strokes, I realized that I could not out-row the fog. *Stay calm,* I scolded myself. I stopped and pulled out the compass. The last time I'd checked, the *Fides* was to the southwest. Rowing that direction was treacherous because the waves came at the dory broadside. I strained to listen. Nothing. I called on my lucky copper. *Please come to my aid now.* I headed southwest. Stroke. Listen. Stroke. Listen. At last, a faint clang seemed to come from the opposite direction. I was heading the wrong way. Or was I? *Should I trust my ears or the compass?* Heavy and unwieldy, the dory rocked as waves hit the side. I listened for another clang. When it came, it was from the southwest. I decided to trust the compass and stayed on my rolly course. Gradually, after much hard pulling, the clang grew louder. At last, a black shape could be seen through the gray. I had found the *Fides*.

Wondering how Orne had fared without his compass, I was overjoyed to see him on deck. Without a word, he grabbed my painter. As if nothing had happened, I pitched my fish aboard and jumped up myself. Orne grabbed my hand as I landed. "Next time, leave a few cod for me," he said. My dory had been perilously full in the rough waves and pea-soup fog. I could have been a goner and Orne knew it.

That night, I climbed into bed in my bulky clothes, pulled up the scratchy blanket, and was grateful to be there. I'd had a close call. If Ma had been there, she would have said, "Jon, learn from your mistakes or you are bound to repeat them." And then she would have waited for me to tell her what I had learned. That night on the *Fides*, I pretended Ma was with me and I told her the day's lessons: *Greed can sink you. Don't let your ears fool you. Keep track of your bearings. Don't panic. Trust your compass.* In my head, I could hear her say, "I'm sure you'll do just fine the next time." And I knew there would be a next time.

ROUTINE SET IN. Our meals were the same day after day. Breakfast was fried halibut. Dinner was fried halibut. For variety, we had baked halibut or baked cod. Occasionally, we ate fried salt pork or boiled salt beef. To break the monotony, it was stewed peas with mince pie or stewed beans with mush and molasses. Tea to drink. I knew just what to expect at the next meal. It was always the same. But I was starving and ate whatever there was. Dorothy's Joe Froggers grew more precious as the weeks passed.

In theory, galley duty was assigned like the watch, but each man had his way of cooking, some of it pretty awful. George had more talent than the rest of us, so most nights he left the splitting to Amos and went to the cookstove.

Captain Perry kept a close eye on the provisions; the food had to last until we got home.

Each of us had our own crockery cup and bowl. First, some warm soup. We balanced it in our hands and downed the broth quickly, before the vessel's roll spilled it. The bowls rarely touched the table. I kept the last drops to give the next course—fish—some flavor. I'd wipe my dish clean with hardtack. We all licked our plates and put them away for the next meal.

Although we were surrounded by seawater, our drinking water was strictly rationed from the barrels we had loaded in Marblehead. I didn't like the murky taste and never brushed my teeth. Orne, Charlie, and George had no teeth to brush. Washing up was pointless and no one shaved. Beards kept faces warm. Mine wasn't full like the Dawsons', but at least some brown stubble covered my chin. A bucket or the rail was the outhouse.

We fished all day, dressed the catch, ate supper, baited the trawls, and then took turns keeping watch. I crawled into bed fully dressed, ready to go again in the morning.

Although every day was the same, no two days were alike. Conditions were constantly changing. Drizzle, fog, sun, downpour, overcast: each changed the color of the sky and ocean. Winds came from every quarter and at every speed. We had dead calm and fearsome squalls. Some days brought a flat sea and others nine-foot waves. The current played havoc with the lines and made the *Fides* swing on her anchor. The combinations were endless. It was a rare but happy day when I could sail downwind to the *Fides* with a plentiful catch under blue sky over a tranquil sea.

I was never bored on the fishing grounds. Schools of porpoise, spouting whales, and flying fish kept us company. We shared the Banks with fishermen from France and Portugal, Maine and Canada. Seeing a schooner from the neighboring town of Gloucester was nice, but meeting another vessel from Marblehead was cause for celebration. The hail of "Bodgo" answered by "Molly Waldo" meant seeing familiar faces and sharing yarns. The crew last in port brought news from home; a vessel expected to sail back first would carry messages and even letters to loved ones.

By mid-September, summer was gone. We wore more layers under our oilskins and another pair of socks inside our boots. We never ventured out in the dories without hats and nippers. Orne and I kept handlining, while the others trawled. On good days, I raised an oar for Orne and he did the same for me.

I'd become a fisherman, but I paid a price. Fish slime and grit caught in my shirt cuffs and chafed my skin into terrible sores. A row of nasty boils rose between my wrists and my elbows. I showed Amos the ugly, painful blisters. "You've got gurry-sores, the mark of a real fisherman," he explained. He showed me how to stake my shirts. I cut off the cuffs and the sleeves to the middle of my forearm. "Your oilskins will still rub your wrists, but at least you can wash the grime off your slicker."

Orne took a look at my sores. "Those boils are ripe and the captain's got to cut 'em open." On top of being a mariner, Perry was the ship's doctor. He pulled a razor from his medical bag and lanced the boils. It hurt like hell. I'd grown tough and didn't cry. When Captain Perry said, "Now you're a blooded Banker," my pride eased the pain.

When the operation was done, Orne slid two copper coils off his arms. "Here. So ya won't get infected." I didn't want to take them. Orne insisted. "I don't need 'em." Orne appealed to the skipper. "Sir, order Bowen to take 'em." Perry nodded. I put the copper around my wrists. *First, the compass. Now his bracelets. It's not quite right,* I thought.

The days became weeks. Captain Perry consulted Orne often about when and where to move for better fishing. Sometimes we'd strike out away from the fleet and sometimes we'd set anchor where others were having good luck. One day in a light fog, I thought my ears were playing tricks. "Bodgo" came across the water. We all listened; it came again. "Bodgo." Bart shouted, "Molly Waldo!" The cry of "Molly Waldo" volleyed back and forth over the water, helping to bring the two vessels closer.

Suddenly, our townsmen popped into view. There was my friend Emmett Bartlett! What a glad exchange of greetings! The *Caroline Jane* had been in the harbor after us, so we asked about the folks back home. Emmett said, "Your mother's flower garden is a sight to see. Dorothy spends half her time over there, helping gather seeds for packets." A month ago, that remark would have made my head jerk, but I just smiled. Emmett went on. "Stumper said, 'If you run into the *Fides*, tell Young Bowen that the gilt rooster crows every morning from out by Half Way.'" Emmett shook his head. "I tell you, poor old Stumper just isn't himself anymore, sending queer messages like that. But I promised to tell you and I've said it!" Before I could respond, the two vessels moved apart. The *Caroline Jane* disappeared into the fog. The visit was over. I wished for home and wondered, *Will our salt ever be wet?*

Even at anchor, we kept night watch. Was the wheel lashed? The anchor holding? We let out cable to keep it from chafing or brought it in when there was too much slack. Our anchor light was a dim candle that was easily blown out by wind gusts. We checked it often, hoping the small flame would keep other vessels away.

Many fishermen had been run down by warships and larger schooners ploughing across the Banks under full sail. Captain Perry complained, "To top that, we have the New York–Liverpool route to contend with." Steamships added a new danger. Under power, freighters and passenger ships crossed the Atlantic, oblivious to the dories and their mother ships. Fog made the situation even more treacherous.

One cold night, I was on watch with Amos. Head cocked to the dark, he stood motionless on the bow, peering into a dense fog. To pass the time, I said, "Amos ..." His raised hand silenced me. A moment later, he swung around and shouted, "Ring the bell!" I ran to sound the alarm. Amos roused the captain. A few minutes later, I heard a deep throbbing. Pretty soon a dark shape loomed up out of nowhere; its towering hulk descended on the *Fides* with terrifying speed.

By then all hands were on deck, shouting and waving. Using wood from the cookstove, Bart and George lit firebrands and hurled them toward the freighter to get its attention. I kept clanging the bell. Charlie lowered a dory as a lifeboat. We braced ourselves for a ram at mid-ships. Then, I heard pistol shots. Captain Perry was firing straight at the bridge of the freighter. Just in time, the steamer veered slightly.

As it passed astern, the steamship almost grazed the *Fides*. "Hang on for your lives!" bellowed Captain Perry. I grabbed the halyards of the foremast and clung tight. The deck tipped violently to the side, as if the *Fides* were heeling under full sail. Loose gear tumbled toward the sea. The port rail dipped underwater. I was sure we would capsize, but then we were thrown the opposite way by the powerful wake of the large ship. "Forget the gear. Save yourself!" yelled Perry. The starboard rail went underwater, crashing down onto the dory. Once more, it seemed we were lost. The next wave rolled the port rail down again; this time we shipped less water. When we rocked back the other way, the rail didn't go under.

Meanwhile, the freighter had disappeared into the fog. Its wake had almost sunk our vessel.

"Orne?" Perry shouted over the ship's tumult.

"Aye, sir!"

"Dawson."

"Here, sir!" The brothers responded in unison.

"Bowen!"

"Yes, sir! On the foredeck, sir!"

Amos and Bart were close by the captain. We were all accounted for. As the rocking eased, we gathered 'round for our orders. "It's a miracle we are in one piece," said Perry. "A couple of tubs of trawl rolled overboard and the gear is a shambles, but we're still afloat … thanks to the watch."

"It was Amos who heard it first," I hurried to inform the captain. The nod that Perry gave my shipmate was more praise than words.

"Not even a dead man could have slept through that infernal clanging," Bart teased. I think he was giving me some of the credit.

"One thing's sure," said Orne. "With fewer fish in our hold, that steamer's wake would've overthrown this vessel. Luckily, it's a good year for fish or the *Fides* would be on the bottom tonight."

"Speaking of the catch," Perry added, "those rollers gave the fare a pretty good shaking. All that rocking settled those splits, leaving lots of room on top. So, let's clean up this mess and get ready for more fishing." Once things were back in place, my shipmates returned to their berths. Tomorrow would dawn early and, like every other morning, we would set out in the dories.

Alone again, Amos and I continued the watch. "Amos ..." I paused but he didn't silence me this time. "How did you hear the engine from so far off?" I hadn't heard it at first.

"'God gave you two ears and one mouth.' My mother used to say that. A lot of good comes from listening." Amos looked up to the heavens. His black eyes were moist. "Mama, you just saved the *Fides*."

Amos had a mother! It came as a surprise. Amos seemed as eternal as time itself. How strange it was to spend so many hours with a man, yet know so little about him.

Casks, rigging, and wreckage floated by.
We suspected that many friends and townsmen had perished.

CHAPTER 8

❧ September Gale ❧

"**A**LL HANDS ON DECK!**"** The order came at 3 o'clock in the morning, a few days later. "Secure the sails!" Although we were at anchor, the wind was blowing the canvas out of the stops. Soon we would have shreds of fabric that were good for nothing. Bart and I worked on the bowsprit to detach the jib. Time and time again, waves washed over us, but finally the big sail was off and we were both back on deck.

Hoping the anchor would hold, we let out 200 fathoms of cable and 30 of chain. The waves built higher and higher in the dark. The *Fides* dragged and held, dragged and held. The yanking on the cable was fearsome. Finally, the captain ordered the anchor up. Everyone took turns on the windlass to retrieve all we'd let out. On the bucking deck, we clung to the ropes for dear life. It was exhausting work, but we spelled each other until it was done.

Bart was on the boom, securing the mainsail, when a huge wave hurled him in the air. As he crashed into the deck, I ran to him, afraid he'd broken his back. Dazed, he got up slowly; it was the only time I saw Tom Barton wince. He climbed right back on the boom and finished the job he'd begun.

We put three reefs in the foresail, leaving just a handkerchief to keep the *Fides* from turning broadside to the mounting seas. Even so, a huge wave washed George and me across the deck. I landed hard against the nest of dories. George was swept to the rail. He grabbed on just in time. Only a miracle kept us both from being washed overboard.

By 4 o'clock, it was howling. Seas broke over the deck without stopping. "Clamp on the fore scuttle," ordered the captain. We secured the hatch to our forward living quarters and everyone huddled in the cabin. We were hove to: our tiny storm sail and the lashed wheel were left to cope with the fury outside.

Treacherous September storms had taken many a schooner and her men. Wedged between two shipmates on the platform, I feared for my life. The howls and whistles sounded like witches and ghosts. Ropes slapped. Every timber strained and groaned. The *Fides* climbed a mountainous wave, piling us on top of each other. I was squashed between Charlie on one side and Amos on the other. Before we knew what happened, we were thrown forward as the vessel pitched down, nose first. One moment, we rode the crest of a tremendous wave; the next, we dashed down its backside. It felt like being thrown from a precipice into a seething, angry pit. Pounding whitewater threatened to crush the *Fides* like an eggshell. We were doomed.

Speechless, we sat pressed against each other, at the mercy of the storm we could not see. But, boy, could we feel it. A monstrous wave struck the vessel from the side. We braced ourselves. With a loud bang, the storm sail jerked to the other side and we were on the opposite tack. Under such stress, the foremast might snap at any moment, leaving a gaping hole for the ocean to pour in. "She's old but seaworthy," Amos had said of the *Fides. How much longer,* I wondered, *can she withstand Nature's wrath?*

My tongue cannot describe the agonizing fear that beset us during those hours. We were compelled to sit idly in that cabin, silently waiting for the inevitable—our destruction. There was not a coward among us. Every man had risked his life to secure the vessel. I was proud to be with these men for my last hour.

Captain Perry stood in the companionway, beneath the battened hatch. He was poised to bolt up on deck, if that would save the ship. With his charts and logbook and sextant, he had guided the *Fides* through all kinds of weather. But Jeremiah Perry had been forced to lash the wheel and put his trust in God. A lump rose in my throat as I watched the tense face of the gruff skipper who put his ship and his crew before himself.

With a nasty, dark bruise rising on his face, Bart was just one step behind the captain. The damage from his violent fall was concealed by his oilskins; the resulting pain was hidden from view. Bart would be the first out in the storm if the captain gave an order. He was somber in those bleak hours. *Will I ever again hear him sing from the masthead?*

To my right were the Dawson brothers. Charlie and George knew horror. They'd been to war, killed for the Union, and carried dead soldiers from the front. Even so, sweat moistened their sideburns. I could not imagine the heavy burden in their hearts. I was anguished just thinking of Ma. The Dawsons had wives and children.

On my left, Amos was alert, ready to spring into action. I'd seen my mysterious watchmate marvel at the stars and use his muscle to fight the power of the wind. Amos never lost touch with miracles and seemed to perform a few himself. But not even Amos could match the force outside our cabin.

Finally, there was Orne. As the *Fides* moaned, his restless hands clenched and unclenched; he seemed to share her agony. A stranger might think him frail, his frame swallowed up by stiff oilskins. But Orne had survived more gales than he could count. But this time, the compass was not around his neck. *If I live through this*, I vowed, *I'll give it back.*

If I live ... If we live ... My shipmates had been strangers to me a month before. In many ways, they were strangers still, but we were bound forever by the hell of this storm.

About noon, a flying timber poked a hole in the deck. Cold saltwater poured into the cabin. It was waist-high. Bedding and clothing were strewn in confusion. Amos raced to the hand pump; by some miracle, it was not blocked. Taking turns, we toiled to keep the water from rising, as waves replaced what we pumped out.

To check the damage, the captain poked his head through the hatch of the companionway. "All hands on deck!" he shouted. We clambered up the ladder. Perry had spotted a light near our bow. Another vessel was headed for us. We could almost touch it with a gaffstaff. A collision seemed certain.

The sea raised the other ship directly above our heads. In the next moment, it would crash down upon us. Charlie, George, Bart, and I started to cut loose the dories that would be our lifeboats. Captain Perry seized a knife and slashed the rope that held the helm. Amos turned the wheel with all his weight. Orne let out our storm sail. The *Fides* veered off in the nick of time to clear the unknown vessel. *What a narrow escape!*

After the sail and wheel were secured anew, we returned to the cabin and the pump. About 6 o'clock in the evening, the wind subsided a little. Bart ventured forward. From the fo'c's'le, he brought back some hard crackers and salt pork—the only food in 24 hours. All night we were battered by the great waves, some 100 feet high. At noon the next day, we went up on deck. The seas were so high, I could hardly stand.

Dory 6 was gone and our foresail was nothing but threads. But we had our vessel and our lives. The *Fides*, apparently, was more fortunate than most. Casks, rigging, and wreckage floated by. We suspected that many friends and townsmen had perished. With great sadness, we set about the grim task of cleaning up the mess. With dread, I watched for any sign of the *Black Hawk* or the *Caroline Jane* ... but saw none.

The rough waves had jostled the 10,000 fish already in the hold,
leaving more room on top for that many again!
So, back to fishing we went.

CHAPTER 9

❧ The Day Nothing Would Bite ❧

A GALE IS NO REASON TO GO HOME. Although a bit soggy, the *Fides* was intact. We pumped and bailed the seawater out. We spread the bedding in the sun. We mended what canvas we could and bent on the spare foresail. After a week, things were straightened out.

Despite the storm, we still had dry salt. In fact, the rough waves had jostled the 10,000 fish already in the hold, leaving more room on top for that many again! So, back to fishing we went. The friendly competition between the trawlers and the handliners continued, but all that really mattered was getting a full fare. With Dory 6 gone, Captain Perry assigned me to Dory 4. I started catching more fish than Old Orne. Maybe some dories *were* lucky after all!

The sunny October days made me retract my vow to return the compass. Giving it back would be awkward. Since that first day of September, we'd never spoken of it. I had not asked Orne about "*Veritas Fides Honorque*," lest I put him on the spot. Stumper would tell me what it meant.

Since the gale, Orne hadn't been himself. He was forgetful. One morning he set out without his bucket of bait. Another without his nippers. I secretly checked his boat when he wasn't looking. Orne always set his anchor near the *Fides* and came back before the others. Maybe that's why I out-fished him. When we dressed the catch, I did most of the salting.

One misty morning in mid-October, mine was the last dory to shove off. I rowed into a northwest wind against a strong current. I hoped both would help carry me back with a full load. Finding a spot that felt right, I set my anchor and put out my lines. The mist was closing in, so I took my bearings. The *Fides* lay to the south, Orne to the southwest. I put the compass inside my shirt and waited.

Nothing would bite. Working at cross-purposes, the current and wind made choppy whitecaps that pitched my dory about. No fish came. I tried a couple of different spots. Nothing. Hours passed. With a handful of fish in my boat, I heard the bell on the *Fides* calling me in. I stowed my anchor and started the long row toward the clang. Never had my haul been so meager.

It got thick. I could barely see a boat length around. Sounds bounced off the fog and played tricks on my ears. When I feathered the oars, I strained to hear anything that might be headed at me. A schooner with her canvas flying or a breaching whale could ram me without warning.

I reckoned I was still a half mile from the *Fides* when a dark shadow appeared off my stern. I paused mid-stroke. Shipping my oars, I fumbled for my foghorn and blew four short toots, the signal for Dory 4. The only reply was the plop of rain, pocking the surface of the sea. I waited and peered where the shadow had been, then blew the horn again. Just rain falling and the clang from the *Fides* behind me.

I took up the oars again and eased backward, with my eyes glued to the spot where I'd seen the shadow. *Is it my imagination or do I really see something?* The current carried a stray oar toward me. I gaffed it in. Faded red and yellow stripes. Orne's colors. A few more cautious strokes. Then, a break in the fog. The orange bow of Dory 5 was just a few yards away.

"Orne!" I yelled. "Old Orne!"

The seat was empty. With clammy hands, I backed toward the dory, grabbed the gunwale, and stared. A round, motionless heap shared the bottom of the boat with a single, large cod.

"Old Orne?!" My voice cracked. I poked him gently, then again, harder. *Please wake up.* But Orne's good luck had run out.

Another clang came from the mother ship. I was alone with the old man and the cod. It was raining in earnest. Water dripped off my sou'wester and mixed with my tears.

With shaking hands, I secured Orne's painter to my stern and started to row. Towing my cargo to the *Fides*, I poured my sorrow into every stroke. By the time I reached the vessel, my tears were spent.

The others had been back long enough to be worried. "There's the boy," I heard Charlie say.

"It's high time you found us," Bart started to tease, but stopped when he saw Orne's boat.

"George, call Captain Perry," Charlie shouted. "Amos, lend a hand."

Amos grabbed my painter. Before you could count to ten, the captain jumped into my dory and scrambled into Orne's. Perry fingered Orne's neck and his wrist. He bowed his head and we all fell silent. The chop didn't allow for more than a moment of respect. Orne's single cod was put aboard and his dory was tied astern, him still in it.

"Pitch up your fish, lad," Perry said. "Orne would want us to salt the catch … what there is of it." He eyed my meager haul. "The trawls didn't catch much either," he said more to himself than to me. "Guess the cod knew something was amiss."

We dressed the sparse catch; each man with his own thoughts. Captain Perry joined me in the hold. "Let's see what you know about salting."

A few splits came down the chute. I covered them with just the right amount of salt. *Not too much and not too little.* Orne's words floated in from Dory 5, where he lay rocking.

After watching me for a while, Perry said, "Seems Orne left the *Fides* a fine salter." That praise was my undoing. "Thank you" caught in my throat and burst out as a moan. My shoulders started to shake.

"We'll miss Old Orne, won't we, Bowen?" The captain's firm hands grasped my upper arms. "I know how you feel, son." His hazel eyes watered, although no tear fell. "On my first voyage, Orne taught me to handline and made me a doryman."

"Really?" I tried to imagine Captain Jeremiah Perry as an apprentice. "You learned to fish from Old Orne?"

"He was just Orne in those days." The captain tried to smile. "Boy, could he find fish ... Did you see that beautiful cod?"

Choked up, I just nodded.

"Orne died doing what he loved, Bowen. He'll be in every line you set and every grain of salt you wet." The dark hold was a smelly place for a eulogy, but it seemed a fitting tribute to the man who had made us both Bankers.

After supper, Bart and Charlie raised Orne's body from the dory. Captain Perry ordered everyone below. There would be no onlookers while he sewed his teacher and friend into a weighted shroud of sailcloth.

At dawn the sea was calm and a light rain fell. We gathered around the oblong bundle, laid on the board that was the seat for Dory 5. I read the 23rd Psalm from my Bible. "Yea, though I walk through the valley of the shadow of death" came out a bit shaky, but I got through it.

Next, the captain spoke solemn words. "We commit the earthly remains of Meriwether Samuel Orne to the Deep—ashes to ashes, dust to dust. From water, all life arises. Mother of Waters, Father of Rain, you have taken back your own. As a stream flows into a river, as a river flows into the sea, may his spirit flow to the waters of healing, to the waters of rebirth."

We raised one end of the plank and eased Orne's body into the sea. "Safe passage," said Captain Perry. The white form sank out of sight, below the restless green. A chorus of "Amen" sent Old Orne on his way.

The Dawsons went to the windlass, Amos and Bart to the halyards, and the captain to the wheel. I took Orne's place on the mainsheet. A gentle breeze carried us away from the spot where the ocean had closed over my friend.

Amos stood beside me in the steady drizzle for a long time. Then, he said, "His was a good life and a good death." His face was calm. "Old Orne was true to himself. Handlining to the end ... and teaching another man to fish. That's not such a bad way to end a life." Orne's passing didn't upset Amos. But he didn't have Orne's compass around his neck. I wanted to share my secret with Amos, but he was still talking. "That psalm was real nice. Orne would have liked it."

I'm sure Amos meant well, but his words made me feel guilty. Since arriving on the Banks, I had not taught him a single letter. I glanced around; no one was within earshot. "I'm sorry, Amos."

"What for?"

I was sorry for a lot of things: for keeping the compass, for Orne's being gone, for failing to teach Amos to read.

"For the lessons." I breathed deep to steady my voice. "I didn't keep my end of our bargain."

"It's not your fault, Bowen. Reading and fishing don't mix." Amos chuckled to himself. "No, they don't mix. Not enough hours in the day."

"But you were getting the hang of it so fast," I insisted. "Maybe back in town ..."

"We'll see. For now, there are fish to catch and miles to cross." Amos was a bit brusque. "Bowen, you have a way of taking things on your shoulders that don't belong there. Reading and fishing just don't mix." There was nothing more to say, so I stared out at the drizzle. It looked like I felt.

Lost in my thoughts, I forgot Amos was still beside me. After a long time, he said, "To tell the truth, I miss those lessons." That's when I knew that one way or another, someday I would teach Amos to read.

WE ANCHORED EARLY THAT DAY and fished from the schooner while there was daylight. Around sunset, Captain Perry called me to his cabin. Bart was already there.

"Bowen, your shipmate has a complaint." With a wide stance, Bart looked cocky. "Ya stole Orne's compass." Bart spit out his accusation. "Twasn't on the body when me and Charlie brought it aboard. Orne always wore that compass. Everyone knows it. Only one alone with 'im was you." Bart's accusing finger nearly poked my chest. "I wager anything it's under your shirt."

Being accused of stealing from a dead man was a hard punch. My mind raced. *Who wouldn't believe Bart? No one knows Orne gave me the compass!* My neck twitched. I wanted to reel back, but held my ground.

"You've heard Bart's claim. Orne's compass was not on his dead body," said Captain Perry matter-of-factly. "When I gathered his effects, it was missing."

"I do have it, sir." I ripped open my collar and showed them the pendant.

"Aha!" Bart crowed. "What did I tell ya?!"

"But Captain Perry, sir," I rushed on, "I didn't steal it, sir. Word of honor."

"Then how did you come by it?" asked the captain.

"Orne gave it to me, sir. On August 31st—the last day we were dorymates."

"That's a good one," Bart scoffed. "What old man would give his compass to a kid?"

"Silence, Tom. Let's hear Jon out." Captain Perry didn't jump to conclusions. "Go on, Bowen."

"He didn't give it to a kid; he was giving it back to an old friend," I countered Bart's challenge.

"How so?" asked Perry.

"Back in '46, Orne had a bet going with my grandpa." I repeated Orne's story about the rivalry, the poker game, the compass trading hands, and my grandfather going down in the gale.

"That's a pretty clever story, Bowen Boy." Bart spit the Bs.

I faced Bart squarely and spoke as calmly as I could. "Bart, it's the honest truth. God is my witness." Unfortunately, I had no other witness. Orne was dead. I turned toward the captain. "With your permission, sir, I'll fetch the Bible and take an oath."

"That won't be necessary. Sit down, both of you." Perry motioned us to the platform. He pulled out his pipe, which meant waiting while he lit it. "Now, this is a peculiar case. Bart, you've been Orne's shipmate for four years, almost five. It's human to covet another man's treasure, especially when that man's got no more use for it. You and Charlie raised Orne out of his dory. You had plenty of time to notice the compass was missing." He took a puff, leaving us to ponder whether that was good or bad.

"Jon, your tale is a good one. A little too good." My heart fell; he thought me a liar. Another puff on his pipe added to my suffering. "As far as I recall, Bowens aren't known for their storytelling. There's just too much truth in your veins to make up a yarn like that." So, Perry believed me! I glanced sideways at Bart; he was fidgeting.

The skipper took a long draw on his pipe before going on. "If Orne *did* give Jon the compass," he pointed at me with the stem of his pipe, "that would solve a riddle that's been bothering me." He had my attention; Bart's, too. "Jon, for a couple of years, Orne's been asking me to sign you. The old man just kept pestering me, saying things like, 'I'd be much obliged if you'd ship the Bowen Boy.' One day, he was really feisty and said, 'Damn it, Perry. I've a debt to pay. I need to settle it with Bowen.'" Perry's pipe went out, so we had to wait while he fussed with it. "I can't imagine Orne owing anything to any man. He was straight as an arrow. But now it's clear. In his mind, he had a debt and was determined to square things while his hands were warm."

Bart seemed to sense the turn this was taking. He was more curious than belligerent when he asked me, "If he gave it to ya, how come ya hid it?"

Why had I? I struggled for an answer. "Having it didn't feel quite right. I even vowed to give the compass back . . .," I said, starting to choke up, "but never did. I was too selfish." My voice was quavering. "If I'd done it, he'd still be with us."

"Bowen, I'll have none of that." The captain was firm. "Don't you dare take credit or blame for Orne's passing. He sensed his time was up and he did what he felt was right. The man settled his affairs, as few men do."

Perry's scolding straightened me out and lifted a weight from me. "Aye, sir," was all I could think to say.

Captain Perry wasn't done. "Before his going, Orne settled another matter." The skipper went to Orne's bunk. "Right after the storm, he came to me and said, 'No one risks his life for a vessel like Tom Barton. When I'm gone, give Bart my knife. He'll know when to use it.'" Captain Perry pulled a leather belt with a sheath from the bunk and handed it to Bart. "Tom, you've earned it."

Bart strapped it on, pulled out the blade, and felt its sharp edge. "Thank you, sir."

"Thank Orne," corrected the captain, "and honor him by using it well."

"I shall, sir." Bart slid the knife back into its case, but kept hold of the carved handle. A moment of silence showed our respect.

"Shake hands," Perry ordered. Bart's grip was strong. Mine, too. The rift between us would heal quickly, I felt sure.

The Fides *pitched in the heavy seas.*
White just kept coming.
Driving snow and sleet had long since soaked through my oilskins.

PLATE 1: *Front Street or Lane to Ferry to the Neck*

PLATE 2: *The Fish Flakes*

PLATE 3: *Waterfront of the Old Town in Fishing Days*

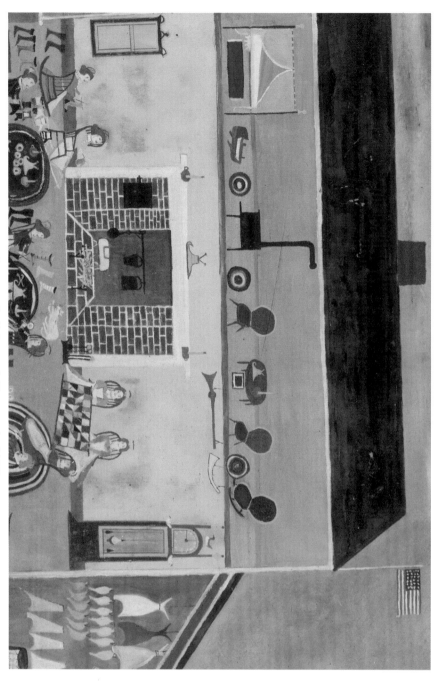

PLATE 4: *Interior of a Fisherman's Home in the Old Days*

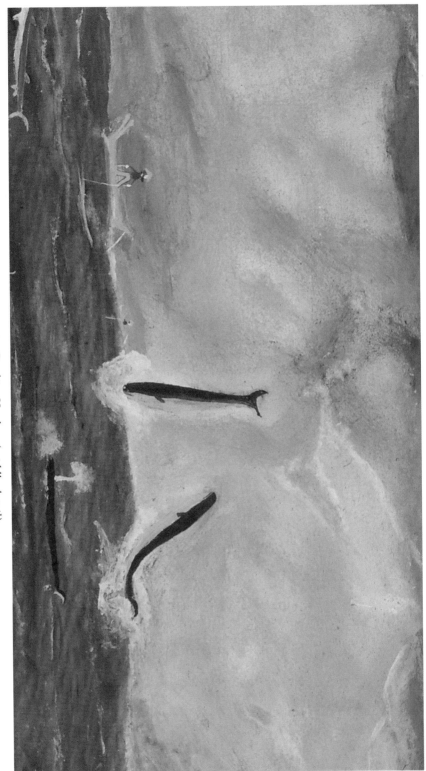

PLATE 5: *Catching Hagdons* (middle detail)

PLATE 6: *Storm of 1868*

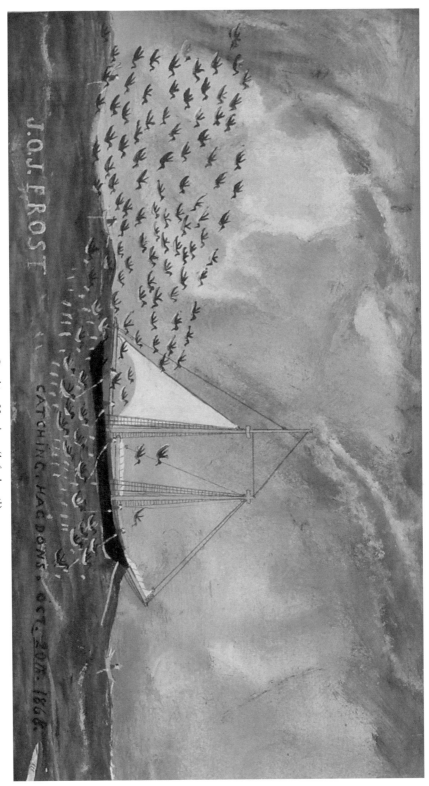

PLATE 7: *Catching Hagdons* (left detail)

PLATE 8: *Parts of Washington, Pleasant and Summer Streets or Pigs Being Driven to Market*

CHAPTER 10

❧ Blizzard on the Banks ❧

THE DAYS GREW SHORTER. Bitter cold set in. A blustery front stirred up whitecaps as far as we could see. Each morning, we set out wearing every layer we had.

About a week after losing Orne, a black cloud covered the sun; mid-morning was dark as night. By mid-afternoon, the captain rang the bell. I arrived first. "Ring in the rest!" he ordered.

"Aye, sir!" As I yanked hard on the lanyard, the first snowflake fell. I stuck out my tongue and tasted winter.

"This is no time for play." Perry was curt as he hurried past. "Ring 'til every man's in." He let out the anchor cable to prevent its chafing and peered out to sea. "Don't stop. It's getting thick fast." Another loud chime told the trawlers where to find us. "Once they're in, go below and fill yourself with hot vittles."

"And the catch, sir?"

"Do as you're told, Bowen. Prepare for what's coming." The furrows deepened on his forehead. "Ice in the rigging will make her top-heavy." He squinted up. I did the same. White flurries hid the masthead. "Even a full hold might not keep her upright."

A blizzard was serious business. Someone would need to clear the rigging as it froze. There were two spars and just one Bart. "You can count on me, sir," I said and hoped it was true.

Perry's hand fell heavy on my shoulder. "Bowen, Fate put you aboard the *Fides* for a reason." His troubled eyes held mine for a moment. Feeling awkward at his closeness, I looked away and saw a dory emerging through the flurries. It was a welcome sight.

"Sir, one boat is in."

"Good. One more to come." Captain Perry strode to grab the painter from George. "Keep ringing, Bowen." His gruff order gave me more comfort than his talk of Fate. Amos started pitching fish. I kept ringing the alarm and watching the dark rigging turn white.

Somehow Bart and Charlie found us in the blinding snow. The last dory was raised and the catch left undressed. The cold would keep the fish fresh. The skipper kept us below until heavy snow forced him to act.

When the order came, Bart handed me an ice pick that he'd readied for the job. "Hack as you go … as best you can," he said before hurrying to the main-mast. I began to step up the windward ratlines of the foremast. With one hand to hold on and one for the pick, I cleared a slippery spot, put my foot on the line where the ice had been, and eased myself upward. It was slow going. Up I went inch by inch, hacking ice off the rigging bit by bit. I heard the crackle of chunks falling, but more white came. The wind whistled. Sleet stung my face. At last, I reached the crosstree. I wrapped my feet into the ropes, leaving my hands free to brush off the snow and ice. Not daring to look down, I hung on as best I could. Chunks flew toward the horizon, never reaching the deck below. I brushed and hacked and brushed and hacked. It was eerie up there alone, with the frozen halyards rattling in an angry chorus.

The *Fides* pitched in the heavy seas. White just kept coming. Driving snow and sleet had long since soaked through my oilskins. My clothes were frigid and stiff. I lost track of time. My teeth chattered, my arms shook, but I had a job to do and kept at it.

The blinding snow was denser than the densest fog. I could see nothing but fuzz below. Muffled shouts seemed to urge me on. "Don't worry," I shouted back, but my holler was carried off by the wind. "I'll keep her upright!" *Keep her upright. Keep her upright. Keep her upright.* My numb arm beat the singsong rhythm. I never felt the pick tumble from my hand. Nor did I hear Charlie yelp as it grazed his cheek.

"**THE SHAKING'S STOPPED,**" said a deep voice. I sank back into oblivion. When I surfaced again, sharp pain shot through my hands. Voices murmured. A body next to me slid away and a scratchy blanket was tucked against my bare skin. Pipe tobacco tweaked my nostrils. I opened my eyes. Captain Perry was leaning over me, a mug in his hands. "Drink this, my boy. It will do you good." His arm slid under my shoulder and raised me to the cup. After a sip, I fell back beneath the covers and slept despite the throbbing in my fingers.

When I next opened my eyes, Bart said, "Sir, he's awake."

The captain and my shipmate towered beside me. *I'm in the captain's berth*, I realized. Pain shot through my hands. "Welcome back, Bowen." Once again, Perry offered a steaming mug. Reaching for it, I discovered cumbersome bandages. I grasped the cup awkwardly and began to remember. "So, she's still afloat?"

"Aye, son."

"We didn't capsize?" I looked from the captain to Bart. "I hacked enough?"

"You hacked too much," said Perry. "You are one obstinate Bowen." Tears welled up. I tried to sip the tea and spilled some. Frustrated, I eyed the rags around my fingers. "Don't worry. You won't be wrapped up long."

Handing back the mug, I asked, "What happened?"

"You've suffered some frostbite, but not too bad. Thanks to Bart. He brought you down." Perry took the mug from my bandaged hands.

"You're a might heavier than ya look," Bart said, shrugging off the praise.

"You came after me?" It seemed impossible. Sending Bart up, Captain Perry had risked the *Fides* and her crew to save me. I was still puzzled.

"Yeah, had to cut ya loose with Orne's knife. In a dead stupor ya was and shakin' like a leaf. Ya didn't heed the captain callin'. Now look at ya."

Perry joined in. "I ordered you to leave it be, but you were mighty determined." The skipper pointed to my hands. "Now you're paying the price. I wish I'd seen the signs sooner."

"But sir, without his stubbornness, we might be goners." Bart's backtalk was out of order, but the captain let it slide.

"All's well that ends well. Go tell the crew that Jon's come around." Bart left me alone with the captain. My fingers throbbed. I winced. "The pain will be pretty tough for a while. We warmed you as much as we could, but you'll suffer some tingling, I'm afraid."

"Will I lose them?" He knew I meant my fingers.

"I hope not. Time will tell."

"Did you ever suffer frostbite, sir?"

He sat down next to me. "I came close once. Eighteen years ago. Aboard the *Prudence*, it was. To avert disaster in a May blizzard, I chipped ice from her rigging. But I was lucky. Another man did half the job."

"Old Orne?"

He laughed. "No, son. Orne was never too good in the rigging. He had a terrible fear of heights."

"Who then?"

"Your pa, Joe Bowen."

For a moment, I forgot the fierce throbbing. "You knew my father?!"

"Knew him … I bunked under him for two years." A smile filled his hazel eyes. "He snored something terrible."

The urge to sleep pulled me under. The last thing I heard was Captain Perry saying, "You Bowens are cut from some mighty fine canvas."

Pride and excitement crowded out the pain in my hands
and the terrible dangers we'd faced. I thrust my shoulders back.
Jon Bowen is coming home from the Banks with a full fare!

CHAPTER

11

✻ *For Home with a Full Fare* ✻

T HE BLIZZARD WARNED OF WINTER. Our provisions
were getting low. The last barrel of drinking water tasted awful. To go
home, we just needed a few more fish.

With my hands in rags, I couldn't row or bait my lines. I wasn't good for
much, but the captain kept me bandaged to reduce the damage to my fingers.
Each morning before setting out in their dories, my crewmates armed me
with handlines and baited hooks. Fishing from the *Fides*, I landed a few cod,
but knew I was far short of my share.

One morning at dawn, Charlie shouted, "The birds!" I looked to windward
and saw quite a sight. The sky was darkened by a black cloud of hagdons
coming in our direction. They had long, slender wings and stubby, black
bodies. Charlie and George grabbed some of the fish livers and scattered them
on the water to draw the birds to the *Fides*. They set to baiting the fish lines.
"Throw them over the side!" Charlie urged me. The hags dove for the livers.
Soon we were pulling them in on the hooks, as if they were fish. We caught
more than 500 birds! And, just like the fish, we dressed and salted them. "My
wife will make many a winter dinner from this catch." Charlie had never been
so cheerful. "You'll get a share, too." Ma would be so pleased. That night, we
ate with gusto. After month upon month of fish, the chewy hagdon was the
most delicious bird I ever tasted.

On the 23rd of October, the *Congress* out of Gloucester anchored close by. Perry rowed over to see how her crew had weathered the storm. He brought back two passengers. We crowded to the rail to see who they were. In the bow was Emmett Bartlett, in the stern Bill Dunn, our townsmen from the *Caroline Jane*.

After handshakes and welcome, we gathered close to hear their harrowing tale. Three shipmates were swept away by a monster wave early on. "At the height of the storm, the captain ordered us to abandon ship," Bill remembered.

Emmett went on. "We got in the dory and rowed like hell. Captain Curtis waited too long. He went down with the *Caroline Jane*."

Bill shook his head as he said, "The Lord saved us that day."

"The next day, the *Congress* found us adrift," Emmett turned upbeat. "Look at us now—aboard the *Fides* from Marblehead.

"Captain Perry said he could use a couple of hands," Emmett said and looked at my bandages. "Seems he meant it."

"Just a little frostbite," I said. My hardship seemed nothing next to theirs.

"Matter of fact, those rags are about to come off." Perry's voice boomed over our chatter. "We're going to need all hands to raise the anchor. Lads, we're going home!"

A great cheer went up. *Home!* I couldn't believe my ears. I slapped Emmett on the back with my padded hands and then unwound the cloths. Swollen and blotchy, with red and white patches of skin, my fingers were tender and tingled. But I didn't mind. I was able to do my share as the *Fides* headed home!

After a hearty supper of warm vittles, we hoisted the main and foresail, sang a chantey, and raised the anchor. Up went the jib. At 6:30 P.M., Captain Perry set a course for home. It was dark, and we drew lots for the watch. Mine would be at midnight, so I crawled into my bunk. I wasn't there for long. At 10 o'clock I heard, "All hands on deck!"

Wanting to get home, the captain had set plenty of canvas flying. The darkness had concealed the storm racing toward us. Now the *Fides* was heeling over ... way too far. There was no time to lose. Charlie, Bill, and Amos had already reefed the main. Next, we had to douse the jib. Bart was waiting at the tip of the bowsprit. Emmett was close behind, balanced on the lines below. They needed another man. During the weeks at sea, I had worked on the bowsprit many times, but never with the *Fides* plunging as she was now.

Never mind. I scrambled out and wrapped my feet into the lines below the 'sprit. Under the water we went again and again, clinging to the ropes and yelling like mad. George grabbed the sheets to control the wild flapping that could knock any one of us into the sea. Amos let the sail down as we wrangled with the monster. In strapping the sail to the bowsprit, I opened the frostbite sores; blood stained the white canvas. After a dreadful hard time, the jib was secure. I moved back on deck. Emmett followed.

Bart was still on the 'sprit when there was a frightening crack. Then another. And another. *Crack! Crack!* The old timber had had enough. Bart and the *Fides* were in danger. As Bart raced aft, a big wave smacked the beam. Bart went flying. By some miracle, he grabbed the edge of the leeward side. Suspended by his fingertips, he could not last long. I threw myself prone on the deck and grabbed his forearms. Pain shot through my hands as the icy saltwater covered the wounds. But it was trivial compared to Bart's peril.

I could not lift Bart's bulk, not even on dry land. He was being pulled and bashed by the waves. I had no traction on the slippery deck. My bleeding hands were slippery. At any moment, I would lose my grip. I must hang on. If swept away, he would be lost.

Just when I felt my hold slipping, a huge weight almost crushed me. Amos pinned me on the deck with his frame. Stretching his arms over mine, he grabbed Bart and heaved. I rolled out of the way as Bart's upper body landed on the deck. I helped Amos drag our shipmate to safety. Bart was barely conscious.

"Bring blankets." The urgent request from Amos scared me. I raced down into the fo'c's'le, grabbed two covers, and was back on deck in a flash. Bart's wet clothes were off and his flesh was blue from the frigid Atlantic. We wrapped him in wool and rubbed his limbs briskly to warm him. "Help me get him into the lee of the nest," Amos said.

"Shouldn't we take him below?" I recalled waking up in the cabin when Bart saved me during the blizzard.

"Captain wants everyone on deck, in case we have to abandon ship." I helped Amos pull Bart into the shelter of the dories.

Downing the sails had reduced our risk of capsizing, but we were still in the teeth of an angry gale. The whistling in the rigging was fearsome. Once again, all could be lost. With a cracked bowsprit, a powerful wind gust could topple the foremast. A falling spar could kill someone or ram a hole in the vessel. Captain Perry stayed at the helm all night. The crew stood by, ready to abandon the *Fides* or save her, if we could. No one went to bed.

As dawn broke, the storm eased and Bart opened his eyes.

"Captain Perry," I called. "Bart's awake."

Charlie took the helm and the captain came over. As he hunched next to my shipmate, I swallowed down tears of relief. Tom Barton had won his battle with the widowmaker.

AFTER THAT STORM, THE BOWSPRIT was weak and hazardous, but we were still afloat and headed for home. Captain Perry was cautious. "Better to get home a day late than not at all," he said. With the main reefed and a small foresail, our progress southwest was slow against the northbound Gulf Stream. With contrary winds and strong currents, sometimes we seemed to make no headway at all. After several frustrating days, a favorable breeze let us unreef the main and sail toward Marblehead on a beam reach.

Soon we saw signs of land: seaweed and driftwood floated by. Occasionally, a land bird would come aboard or alight on the rigging. Bart recovered quickly and seemed unfazed by his close encounter with death. No one could stop him from scrambling up the mainmast and scanning the horizon. At last, 17 days after leaving the Banks, Bart shouted, "Land, ho!"

"Where away?" asked the skipper.

"Two points off the starboard bow."

I raced to the foredeck. Amos pointed to the horizon. "Looks like a dark cloud," I replied, not wanting my hopes to be dashed. Amos said nothing to convince me otherwise, but the smile in his black eyes told me land was a sure thing. Pride and excitement crowded out the pain in my hands and the terrible dangers we'd faced. I thrust my shoulders back. *Jon Bowen is coming home from the Banks with a full fare!*

Rip … Rip … Rip … My jacket burst, just as Mr. Dalton had said it would. To celebrate, I pulled the last ginger cookie from my duffle. I found Emmett amidships. "Look what I've got," I crowed.

"Well, I'll be," Emmett grinned. "It's one of Dorothy's Froggers!"

"Saved it just for this occasion," said I and gave him a big piece. Looking up, I shouted to Bart at the masthead. "Come on down!" I waved the cookie to tempt him.

"No. You come up, Bowen," he laughed. Could the old spar take the weight of both of us?

From his spot at the wheel, Captain Perry gave a nod. "The *Fides* is on her last run for home. She won't fail me now." I had no excuse to stay on deck. Cookie in hand, I climbed the ratlines straight up to the crosstree without hesitation. Bart moved to the leeward side of the mast, leaving the windward spot for me. The sun was setting behind Cape Ann. What a view!

I split the rest of the Frogger in two and gave Bart the larger half. "Thanks, Bowen. You're alright." He bit into the soft, sweet dough. We stood side by side—rum and ginger on our tongues, wind in our hair, home in sight.

When the last crumb was gone, we returned to the deck. With one more tack, the *Fides* was headed straight for Marblehead. One by one, my ship-mates disappeared below and emerged looking presentable. After weeks with too little water and too little time, I washed my face and brushed my teeth. I was proud of my full beard and trimmed it the way Bart trimmed his.

Anticipation grew. We were all on deck when—*bump!*—the *Fides* shud-dered. Everyone froze. After a second bump, we sailed on. We had grazed the Southern Breaker! High tide is all that saved us from disaster on the rocky ledge, so close to home.

During the long sail from the Banks, I had kept imagining my home-coming. When someone in town spotted a sail on the horizon, the whole town would crowd onto the Point O' the Neck, the wharves, and the roof-tops. Ma would be there, waving. Dorothy might be with her. I wondered if Dorothy knew that the *Caroline Jane* had sunk. She would be overjoyed to see Emmett.

As night fell, I realized our arrival would be uneventful. No one would see us coming. There would be no hero's welcome, just a stealthy arrival under the cover of darkness. It was pitch-black when we came to anchor at 10 P.M. in Marblehead Harbor. On the shore, there was not a soul or a light in sight. All the townsfolk were in bed.

We climbed into the dories and rowed to the wharf. It was plenty cold, being the 10th of November. Emmett and I walked up Front Street. His doorway came first. He rapped loudly. *Ta ta ta ta ... ta ta.* We'd used that code as kids. Dorothy flung the door open and leaped into her brother's arms. He lifted her up and spun her around. Dorothy sang out with joy. "Mother! Mother! Emmett's here!" She dragged him into the house. Seeing their happy reunion made me impatient for my own.

A few steps later, I knocked and shoved open the heavy door of home. Ma heard and came running. What a happy meeting! Will was there, too! The *Black Hawk* had come home with all its crew.

Of course Ma eyed my hands first thing. "Just a little frostbite, nothing to worry about," I said. She would inspect my wounds in the morning and make me go to see Doctor Thompson.

Ma cried when I told her about Old Orne, but she liked the part about my reading the 23rd Psalm. Will couldn't take his eyes off the compass; he turned it over and over between his rough fingers.

There was so much to tell. It was nearly morning before I got to bed. I slept like a log and when I got up it seemed so strange not to feel any pitching and rolling. Ma had a hot breakfast ready, and how good it did taste.

AFTER BREAKFAST, I WALKED UP Ferry Lane to see Stumper. *First, I'll tell him how I can handle a dory and pitch fish and climb the ratlines. Only after that will I tell him how I can navigate. That's when I'll reveal the compass.*

As I neared the shoe shack, I stopped. No witch ball swirled in the sun. Some old boards were nailed across the window. A padlock held the door shut tight. "Stumper's gone," a neighbor said. "The last storm was too much for him. Never woke from it."

Not knowing what to say, I said nothing and turned away. In a few steps, I reached the bluff overlooking the harbor. It was a blur. *Stumper gone. It can't be.* It was Stumper who had sent me out to the Banks with a store of luck that lasted clear through to the end. It was Stumper who would relive my adventures with his wrinkly grin egging me on to tell more. And it was Stumper who would know what those words meant: *Veritas Fides Honorque.*

In my pocket, I fingered the little cloth bag with the faded yellow tie that had held three copper coins. Inside was the compass that Stumper would never see. I pulled out the pendant and turned it over. *Veritas Fides Honorque.*

A wave crashed on the rock below. *Veritas.* As the water pulled back, I heard, "Truth." A moment later, another wave broke. *Fides.* "Trust" reached my ear as the water receded. One more breaking wave. *Honorque.* "And honor," Stumper's voice filled my head. "Truth, trust, and honor. That's all you need to steer straight." Slowly, I looped the chain around my neck. Looking beyond the lighthouse to Half Way, I remembered the clink of two coppers hitting their mark … and the splash of a third falling into the sea.

From Ferry Lane, I went to the wharf and rowed to the *Fides*. I fetched my duffle, my share of hagdons, and my garner. The odd collection of fish fins and tongues were not worth selling but would supplement my family's larder.

That afternoon I went up Washington Street to see my friends. I could scarcely walk, as I still had my sea legs on. Since leaving in August, I'd gained 25 pounds. I could whip any boy in town. Well, maybe any boy except Bart.

At the head of the street, Dorothy and her friend Abigail were beating hoops. Rolling the metal band toward me, Dorothy called out, "Jon. Jon." She passed the hoop to Abby and shook my hand. "You brought Emmett home! Mother thought he was a ghost. We knew that the *Caroline Jane* went down, but I never gave up hope." Dorothy was bubbling over with happiness.

"The Joe Froggers . . ." I began.

"Emmett told me. You saved one for the very last day!" Dorothy was pleased. "Next year, we'll make you a double batch. Won't we, Abby?"

Always shy, her friend hung back, but I noted her chestnut hair shining in the sun. Holding my head high and steady, I couldn't suppress a grin. Dorothy urged her forward and finally Abby shook my hand. "Welcome home, Jon." Her hand was small and soft and warm against my rough skin. *So, this is how it feels to be home from the Banks!*

AT DAWN THE NEXT DAY, streaks of pink and gray filled the sky as I rowed to the *Fides*. The first rays of sunlight bounced off Stumper's shack on the bluff. A piercing crow broke the quiet. Perched proud on the roof was a rooster. A new day had begun.

To collect the $20 due me, there was one more task I had to do—unload the splits from the hold of the *Fides*. All day the crew toiled at washing out. We lashed a wooden pound next to the vessel and dumped the splits into it. Rinsing the fish in the harbor removed the excess salt. From the pound, we filled our dories and rowed to the beach, where carts were waiting. This time, two boys, Enoch and Philip, would haul the splits to the flakes ... not me! Our catch soon covered the racks that sprawled over the hills, headlands, and the Neck. It was a fine showing for the entire town to see.

When the pound was empty, Captain Perry called everyone on deck. "Men, we've done well. Our fare will fetch a good price. The misfortunes of others have increased the demand for our catch. Let us remember our lost townsmen and thank the higher powers that brought us home." We bowed our heads. "Amen," said Perry, and we echoed him.

His commander's voice returned. "Next April, I'll take the helm of the *Oceana*. She's ready in Essex. God willing, her maiden voyage will be six months. Do you want to ship with me?"

Captain Jeremiah Perry did not have to ask twice. Charlie shook his hand first, followed by his brother. Amos was right behind. Bart was next. "You'll be a sharesman, Tom." Bart grabbed Perry's hand and pumped it. "Save that grip for the *Oceana*," the captain teased. Finally, it was my turn. "Bowen ... I'll need a navigator. Be sure to bring that compass."

We shook hands all around, said goodbye, and climbed into our dories. As I rowed ashore, snowflakes fell. We were home just in time. Winter was here. But never mind. Come April, we'd go overland to Essex to bend on the crisp, new sails. Before long, we'd be together again, taking the *Oceana* to the Banks for her first fare. And next year, I would teach Amos to read!

❧ Glossary ❧

To AID READERS' UNDERSTANDING, this glossary explains the way that many terms are used in this story. More technical definitions or alternative meanings for these words may be appropriate in other contexts.

A Few Expressions Used by Marblehead Fishermen

"Bending on a sail": To secure a sail by fastening or tying with a knot. Used when putting a sail on a ship for the first time; for example, when the vessel is launched in the spring or to replace a ripped sail.

"Dousing the jib": Taking down the big triangular sail at the front of the boat.

"Dressing the fish": To process the fish that have been caught, by cutting off the heads, removing the inner parts, splitting them in two, and salting them.

"Gaffing a fish aboard": Using a long pole with a sharp hook to haul a fish onto the boat.

"Ganging the hooks": Tying the branch lines and hooks onto the ground line of a trawl.

"Getting the wet out": Drying the split fish in the sun back on land.

"Nest of dories": A stack of rowboats on the deck of the schooner.

"Reefing the main": Reducing the amount of canvas exposed to the wind.

"Sounding the bottom": Throwing a special rope with lead weights to measure the depth of the sea.

"Staking a shirt": Cutting the cuffs off of shirtsleeves at mid-forearm to prevent sores.

"When the salt is wet": When the hold is full of fish and the crew can head home.

Glossary of Terms Used in *Molly Waldo!*

aft: Toward the back of a ship.

aloft: High above the deck, in the rigging of a sailing ship.

amidships: Toward the middle of the ship.

awl: A pointed tool for making holes in leather. (Used by Stumper for shoemaking.)

bait-butt: A wooden box that was a survival kit for a doryman. Contents might include a small foghorn, water pouch, spare nippers, tobacco, and hardtack.

beam: The width of a vessel at its widest point. (In the case of the *Fides*, this is about the midpoint of its length.) In a **beam reach**, the wind is at 90 degrees to the keel or the line that runs from bow to stern. (The word "beam" is also used to refer to some of the wooden parts of the *Fides*, including the bowsprit.)

bed tick: A bag made of flour sacks or canvas filled with straw and used as a bed.

belaying pin: A removable wooden pin fitted in a hole in the rail of a boat to secure ropes; a type of cleat. (Also used by Orne and Jon to club large fish to be able to bring them into the dory.)

bend on: To attach or fasten (as in "bend on a sail").

berth: A bunk on a ship, used for sleeping.

"Bodgo": The cry Marbleheaders used to greet another vessel from the town.

boom: A long spar extending aft from a mast to hold the bottom edge of a sail.

bow: The front end of a ship.

bowsprit (also **'sprit**): A long spar extending out from the bow of a ship to support the stays of the foremast.

block: A pulley; a wheel on an axle around which a rope can run to apply force. (On the *Fides*, wooden blocks control the sails.)

cabin: An enclosed space on a boat that serves as shelter and living quarters. (On the *Fides*, the cabin is in the stern and houses the captain and sharesmen.)

canvas: The cloth from which sails were made. Also used to refer to the sails (as in "The *Fides* had all her canvas flying" or "we need to reduce the canvas").

chart: A nautical map—a graphic representation of an area of the ocean, showing the coastline, land formations, and the depth of the water. (The charts on the *Fides* were not as accurate or detailed as those of today, but they were still critical tools for navigation.)

compass: A navigational instrument that shows the direction in which the ship is going.

compass rose: The face of the compass, marked with north, south, east, and west (and often additional points and/or degrees). A needle that rotates and provides the direction relative to Earth's poles.

crosstree: A horizontal bar near the top of a mast that is attached to the shrouds and contributes to supporting the mast.

cut-tail: A boy working on a fishing schooner who was paid only for the fish he actually caught. To keep track of his catch, he cut the tails off.

dory: A small, narrow rowboat with a flat bottom and high sides. The dories were stacked on the deck of the fishing schooner in a "nest" and launched for fishing.

douse: To take in or lower a sail.

fare: A specific voyage to catch fish (as in "on Jon's first fare to the Grand Banks"). Also, the size of the catch on a voyage (as in "they came home with a full fare").

fathom: A unit of length equal to six feet, used to measure the depth of water.

flake: A wooden platform on land where split fish were laid in the sun to dry.

forecastle (also **fo'c's'le**): The area below deck in the forward part of a vessel where the meals were cooked and some of the crew slept. (On the *Fides*, Jon slept in the fo'c's'le; the captain and sharesmen slept in the cabin.)

foremast: The forward mast on a schooner.

foresail: The sail attached to the foremast and positioned between the two masts. This sail was often made smaller by reefing to serve as a storm sail.

forestay: A cable extending from the head (top) of the foremast to the bowsprit.

freeboard: The height above the water level of a ship's deck or gunwale.

furl: To fold and tie a sail to take it down (as in "to furl the jib").

gaff: The pole (spar) that runs along the top of a sail, making it four-sided rather than triangular. (The *Fides* is a gaff-rigged schooner; the foresail and the mainsail run fore and aft and each have a gaff at the top edge.)

gaffstaff: A long pole with a sharp hook on the end, used to haul fish aboard (as in "to gaff the fish aboard").

gait: The speed at which the ship is traveling.

galley: The area on a ship where food is prepared (the kitchen).

gangings: Branch lines off a trawl line, each with a hook at the end.

garner: A collection, store, or supply of something. (Used for the fisherman's share of fish parts that could not be sold, but could be used to feed his family.)

gimbal: A device that permits an object, such as a compass, table, or stove, to remain level or vertical despite the movement of the ship. (On the *Fides*, the cookstove is gimbaled.)

gunwale (pronounced "gunnel"): On a rowboat or dory, the upper edge of the side. (If water comes over the gunwale, then water is entering the boat.) So named because the guns were mounted in a comparable location on warships.

gurry-sores: Blisters that develop on a fisherman's arms when the fish slime and grit rub into the skin and make open sores that can easily become infected.

hagdon (also **hag**): A species of sea bird, also known as a *shearwater*.

halyard: A rope used to raise or lower a sail.

handlining: Fishing with a line held over the side of the boat, with only one or two hooks per line.

hardtack: A biscuit made with only flour and water, sometimes called a *sea biscuit*.

head: The top (of a mast) or upper edge or corner (of a sail).

header: The fisherman who cuts the head off when dressing the fish.

heel: To tilt to one side; used to describe the motion of a sailboat due to the wind blowing on the sails. (The *Fides* heeled over when her sails were full of wind.)

helm: The steering mechanism of a ship. (On the *Fides*, this is a wheel.)

hogshead: A large barrel of 60 gallons or more. Salt came in hogsheads.

hold: A part of a ship, below the decks, where the fish are stored.

hoops: The circular bands of metal put around a barrel to hold it together. (The bands were used for a game in which the rings were rolled with a stick, called "beating hoops.")

hove to (past tense of **heave to**): a way of setting small sails and/or the helm in a storm so that the boat moves slowly ahead but does not have to be steered. (The *Fides* was hove to in the September gale.)

hull: The body of a ship (exclusive of its masts and rigging).

jib: A triangular sail, supported by the forestay, that runs from the head of the foremast to the bowsprit.

Joe Froggers: Spicy molasses cookies, the size of lily pads, that were first baked by Black Uncle Joe and later by the women of Marblehead. These treats would stay fresh during the long sea voyages.

keel: The "backbone" of a ship, which runs lengthwise along the bottom from bow to stern and supports the frames that shape the hull.

leeward: On or toward the side of a ship that the wind crosses second. On a sailing ship, the leeward side is the "low" side when the boat heels over.

logbook (also the **log**): A book for navigational notes, such as location, distance traveled, weather conditions, etc. (On the *Fides*, the logbook is kept by the captain.)

log line (also the **log**): A rope with knots in it that is used to measure the speed at which the ship is traveling. (Amos teaches Jon to measure the ship's gait—to use the log line—and report it to the captain.)

longlining: Fishing with a ground line laid on the sea bottom with many branch lines with baited hooks (gangings); also called trawling. Trawling methods today involve dragging a net through the water.

mainmast: The taller mast on a sailing ship. (On the *Fides*, this is the aft mast.)

mainsail: The sail attached to the mainmast. (On the *Fides*, this sail is larger than the foresail and is gaff-rigged.)

mainsheet: The rope that controls the position of the mainsail relative to the wind.

mast: A vertical pole (spar) that rises from the keel and supports the sails and rigging on a sailboat.

masthead: The top of a mast.

mastheadman: A crewmember who stands near the top of the mast on a sailing ship to serve as a lookout. (Bart is the mastheadman on the *Fides*.)

Neck: An island across from the mainland of Marblehead; the two shores form Marblehead Harbor. At low tide, you can walk across a sandbar to reach the Neck. Today, a causeway connects the Neck to the rest of Marblehead and closes one end of the harbor. Before the road was built, a ferry crossed the harbor. The ferry dock on the Neck and an early lighthouse on the point both appear in several Frost paintings.

nippers: Sturdy wool rings that fit around the palms to protect the hands from cold, cuts, and rope burns while leaving the fingers free for baiting hooks.

painter: A rope attached to the bow of a boat, to secure or tow it.

pens: Boxes that were set up on the deck to hold the fish before they were dressed.

point: To bring the bow of a sailboat close to the direction from which the wind is blowing (as in "to point into the wind"). When sailing, to point is to sail as nearly into the wind ("as close to the wind") as the sails will permit. Pointing is synonymous with being close hauled or "on the wind."

port (side of a ship)**:** The left-hand side of a ship when facing forward.

pound: A floating box that was tied beside the vessel upon returning to the harbor. The salted splits were dumped into the pound to wash the excess salt out.

rail: The horizontal frame or edge of a ship. The rail runs around the top of the hull and marks the outer edge of the deck.

ratlines: Thin lines tied between the shrouds to form a ladder to permit the crew to go aloft to handle the sails, make repairs, or be a lookout.

reach: The point of sail when the wind is coming across the side of the boat. In a beam reach, the wind is at 90 degrees to the keel or the line that runs from bow to stern.

reef: To reduce the surface area of a sail by lowering the canvas part way and tying it to the boom in order to make the boat more stable in windy conditions.

rigging: All the apparatus that moves a sailboat forward, including the spars, sails, shrouds, and ropes that make up the upper structure of the vessel.

salter: The member of the crew who adds the salt to the dressed fish when packing them in the hold. This is a critical job because too much or too little salt can make the whole catch worthless.

sandglass: An instrument for measuring time, by which sand flows from one glass chamber to another in a fixed amount of time; also called an hourglass.

schooner: A sailing ship with at least two masts. (The *Fides* is a two-masted schooner with the forward mast being shorter than the mainmast.)

scuttle: The structure over an opening in the deck that keeps water out but allows people to come and go (except in the worst conditions). (On the *Fides*, the cover for the forecastle, the *fore scuttle*, was closed only in gale conditions.)

sextant: A navigational instrument used for measuring the altitudes of celestial bodies to determine a ship's position at sea.

sheer: The upward curve of a vessel's longitudinal lines as viewed from the side.

sheet: A rope that controls the position of a sail relative to the wind.

sharesman: A member of the crew who receives a portion of the profits based on the income from the catch minus the outflow of ship's expenses.

shrouds: The ropes or wire cables stretched from the masthead to the sides of a vessel to support the mast.

skate: A 50-fathom ground line used for trawling, with branch lines for hooks every six feet.

sou'wester: A waterproof oilskin hat with a very broad, slanted brim at the back, worn by seamen. Also used to refer to an oilskin slicker with buckles, worn in rough weather.

spar: A wooden pole, used to support sails and rigging. (Spars on the *Fides* include the masts, booms, gaffs, and bowsprit.)

splits: The name given the fish that have been cut in half down the middle. The **splitter** did this important job; a clean cut meant a higher quality product and a higher price for the catch.

starboard: The right-hand side of a ship when facing forward.

stay braces: The rods that run from the end of the bowsprit down to the waterline, to support the bowsprit.

stay: A rope or wire cable used to support a mast or spar.

stern: The rear end of a ship.

tack: The course of a sailboat relative to the wind. As a verb, the act of changing from port tack to starboard tack or vice versa. (On port tack, the wind comes over the port side of the ship; on starboard tack, the wind comes over the starboard side.) Also means the lower forward corner of a fore-and-aft sail.

throater: The fisherman who cuts the throat of the fish and takes out the livers (after it has been decapitated by the "header").

trawl: The equipment used to catch fish with a long line with many branch lines with baited hooks. As a verb, to fish in this manner.

trawling: Fishing with a ground line laid on the sea bottom with many branch lines with baited hooks (gangings); also called longlining. Trawling methods today involve dragging a net through the water.

tub: A wooden bucket holding the trawl lines or handlines for fishing.

vessel: A ship, usually of some size. (In *Molly Waldo!*, the term "vessel" is used for the schooners and other large ships, not the dories.)

widowmaker: The nickname given to the bowsprit by fishermen because so many men were lost when working out on this long spar to douse the jib.

winch: A stationary hand-powered machine used for hoisting or hauling, having a drum around which rope or chain is wound that is attached to the load (a sail or anchor) being moved.

windlass: A special type of winch used to raise the anchor by turning a drum around which the anchor line or cable is wrapped.

windward: On or toward the side of a ship that the wind crosses first. On a sailing ship, the windward side is the "high" side when the ship heels over.

❧ *Recipe for "Joe Froggers"* ❧

I N THE REVOLUTIONARY WAR DAYS, a free black man named Joseph Brown ran a tavern on the edge of a frog pond on Gingerbread Hill in Marblehead. His molasses cookies were the best in town and as big as the lily pads where the frogs sat. Marblehead fishermen took the sweets on their long voyages to the Grand Banks; the rum and molasses kept the Froggers moist for months. After Black Joe died, the tradition was kept by the wives of the fishermen with debate and rivalry about the best way to make "Joe Froggers." We offer this recipe that creates a smaller cookie, but is otherwise true to the sweets that went to sea.

❈ Joe Froggers ❈

(Yields about 2 dozen cookies)

Combine	2 teaspoons baking soda with 2 cups dark molasses *Mix well and set aside.*
Measure	1 cup rum (or ½ cup hot water and ½ cup dark rum) *Set aside.*
Mix	½ teaspoon each cinnamon and allspice 1 teaspoon each powdered clove and nutmeg 1 tablespoon ginger 2 teaspoons salt (sea salt preferred)
Add	The spice mixture to 2 cups granulated sugar
Cream	½ cup margarine and ½ cup butter with the sugar mixture
Sift	7 cups flour

Combine the flour to the sugar mixture, alternatively with the rum and the molasses mixture, beating well after each addition. Do this in 2 or 3 rounds. Dough will be sticky.

Divide the dough into 3 parts and form each into a ball. Moisten each ball with rum and wrap in waxed paper. Chill overnight in the refrigerator.

Roll the balls one at a time to ¼ inch thick on a well-floured surface. Flour the dough, surface and rolling pin often. Cut with a large round cutter—4 to 5 inches in diameter. (Keep dough in the refrigerator until you are ready to roll it.)

Bake on a lightly buttered cookie sheet in a 375°F oven for about 10-12 minutes.

To prevent breakage, let stand a few minutes before removing from sheet.

Place in storage jar when cool.

ENJOY!

Bibliography

Language from the following archival materials is woven through *Molly Waldo!* as descriptions and/or dialogue.

Damon, Frank C. Various articles in the *Salem Evening News*, c1920s. (Found as clippings in scrapbooks compiled by J.O.J. Frost.)

Frost, John Orne Johnson. "The Life of a Unique Character in a Unique Town (lovingly typed by his granddaughter Ethel N. Frost)," 1928.

Proctor, Captain John. Recollections of the Great Gale of 1846 are captured in an interview with the *Boston Sunday Globe*, originally published in 1890.

Roads, Jr., Samuel. *The History and Traditions of Marblehead*. Boston, MA: Houghton, Osgood and Company, 1880. (Includes memories of Captain Thomas J. Peach, a Marblehead skipper who sailed to the Banks for 50 years, making 85 voyages.)

Snellen, Captain Charles H. "How the Gerry Engine Company's Gilt Rooster Went to Sea" and other yarns. (Within a clipping entitled "Short Sea Stories Told by Fishermen of Old Marblehead," found in Scrapbook #2 compiled by J.O.J. Frost, c1924.)

The following books, films, and websites inspired and validated the story told in *Molly Waldo!*

Cridland, Claudia E. Skerry. "Old Burial Hill: Marblehead, Massachusetts." http://freepages.genealogy.rootsweb.ancestry.com/~ccridland/index.htm?

Damon, Frank C. "Daily Life aboard a Marblehead Fishing Smack by 'D' [1838]." Published in the *Salem Evening News*, 1926.

Fisher, Captain R. Barry. *A Doryman's Day*. Gardiner, ME: Tilbury House Publishers; and Bath, ME: Maine Maritime Museum, 2001.

Garland, Joseph E. with Captain Jim Sharp. *Adventure: Last of the Great Gloucester Dory-Fishing Schooners*, 2nd edition. Gloucester, MA: The Curious Traveller Press, a division of The Pressroom Printers, 2000.

"Glossary of Nautical Terms." *Wikipedia*. http://en.wikipedia.org/wiki/Glossary_of_nautical_terms

Hudson, Richard. "Notes on Sailing Small Schooners." http://www.issuma.com/rhudson/RR/SchoonerSailingNotes.htm

Kipling, Rudyard. *Captains Courageous: A Story of the Grand Banks*, 1897. Originally appeared as a serialization in *McClure's*, starting in the November 1896 edition.

Kurlansky, Mark. *Cod: A Biography of the Fish That Changed the World*. New York: Penguin Books, 1997.

Kurlansky, Mark. *The Last Fish Tale: The Fate of the Atlantic and Survival of Gloucester, America's Oldest Fishing Port and Most Original Town*. New York: Riverhead Books, 2008.

Peterson, Pam. *J.O.J. Frost: A Gallery Guide*. Marblehead, MA: Marblehead Historical Society, 2003.

Peterson, Pam Matthias. *Marblehead Myths, Legends and Lore: From Storied Past to Modern Mystery*. Charleston, SC: The History Press, 2007.

Seltzer, David, and George Sluizer. *Lonely Dorymen: Portugal's Men of the Sea*, a National Geographic Society Special, 1968. Videos can be viewed at: http://www.fishingunited.com/forum/viewtopic.php?f=38&p=35987#p35955

Vogler, Christopher. *The Writer's Journey: Mythic Structure for Writers*, 3rd edition. Studio City, CA: Michael Wiese Productions, 2007.

Works by the following artists provided visual inspiration.

Craske, Leonard (sculptor)

> ❦ *Man at the Wheel*, also known as *Gloucester Fisherman's Memorial*, 1925. Gloucester Harbor, Gloucester, MA

> ❦ *They Also Serve Who Stand and Wait: Portrait of a Fisherman's Wife*, c1944. Cape Ann Museum, Gloucester, MA (Craske created this model for a companion statue for *Man at the Wheel*. His statue of the woman waiting was never erected; the Pike statue mentioned below is the memorial that now stands to honor the wives.)

Frost, John Orne Johnson (painter and historian known as J.O.J. Frost)

> ❦ The paintings, models, and sculptures (c1920s) in the Marblehead Museum and Historical Society were the original inspiration for this story.

Homer, Winslow (painter)

> ❦ *Eight Bells*, 1886. Phillips Academy, Addison Gallery of American Art, Andover, MA

> ❦ *The Fog Warning*, 1885. Museum of Fine Arts, Boston, MA

Hoyne, Thomas Maclay (painter)

> ❦ *First for Home*, 1978

> ❦ *The Mastheadman*, 1984

> ❦ *The Widowmaker*, 1979

Pike, Morgan Faulds (sculptor)

> ❦ *The Gloucester Fishermen's Wives Memorial*, 2001. Gloucester Harbor, Gloucester, MA. Erected in lieu of the Craske sculpture *They Also Serve Who Stand and Wait*.

List of Paintings by J.O.J. Frost

THE PAINTINGS IN THIS BOOK are all works of John Orne Johnson "J.O.J." Frost (1852-1928) from the collection of the Marblehead Museum and Historical Society.

J.O.J. Frost viewed himself as a historian rather than an artist. The images featured in this book come from larger works that he created using house paint on wooden boards in the 1920s. The original paintings listed in this index can be seen by visiting the J.O.J. Frost Folk Art Gallery in Marblehead, Massachusetts.

The authors thank the Marblehead Museum and Historical Society for permission to use these pictures that inspired the writing and publishing of *Molly Waldo!*

Images Reproduced for Cover and Front Matter

A Bird's Eye View in 1867
46.5" X 71.25"   MHS # 1931.864

J.O.J. Frost with Carved and Painted Cod
Photograph by Fred Litchman, c1920s   MHS # 1996.156.01

Map of the Grand Banks and North Atlantic
Compilation by Marblehead Museum and Historical Society,
adapted by Peri Poloni-Gabriel, Knockout Design

Paintings Reproduced as Colored Plates
In some cases, a detail is taken from the larger painting.

PLATE 1: *Front Street* or *Lane to Ferry to the Neck*
24.5" X 46.75"   MHS # 1931.865

PLATE 2: *The Fish Flakes*
17.75" X 46.25"   MHS # 1931.842

PLATE 3: *Waterfront of the Old Town in Fishing Days*
26.75" X 30.75"   MHS # 1931.857

PLATE 4: *Interior of a Fisherman's Home in the Old Days*
22" X 45.5"   MHS # 1931.804

PLATE 5: *Catching Hagdons* (middle detail)
11" X 64.75"   MHS # 1931.853

PLATE 6: *Storm of 1868*
19.75" X 46.5"   MHS # 1931.867

PLATE 7: *Catching Hagdons* (left detail)
11" X 64.75"   MHS # 1931.853

PLATE 8: *Parts of Washington, Pleasant and Summer Streets* or
Pigs Being Driven to Market
22 3/16" X 27 13/16"   MHS # 1931.849

Paintings Reproduced as Black and White Images
at the Beginning of Chapters of *Molly Waldo!*

CHAPTER 1: *The Fish Flakes* (detail)
17.75" X 46.25"   MHS # 1931.842

CHAPTER 2: *A Bird's Eye View in 1867* (detail)
46.5" X 71.25"   MHS # 1931.864

CHAPTER 3: *Waterfront of the Old Town in Fishing Days* (lower detail)
26.75" X 30.75"   MHS # 1931.857

CHAPTER 4: *Waterfront of the Old Town in Fishing Days* (upper detail)
26.75" X 30.75"   MHS # 1931.857

CHAPTER 5: *Catching Hagdons* (right detail)
11" X 64.75"   MHS # 1931.853

CHAPTER 6: *Catching Hagdons* (middle detail)
11" X 64.75"   MHS # 1931.853

CHAPTER 7: *Going Aboard*
19.5" X 29"   MHS # 1931.828

CHAPTER 8: *Storm of 1868* (detail)
19.75" X 46.5"   MHS # 1931.867

CHAPTER 9: *Homeward We Go*
11" X 18.5"   MHS # 1931:836

CHAPTER 10: *Snow Storm on the Banks—May 3, 1869*
11 3/8" X 36"   MHS # 1931.832

CHAPTER 11: *Goodwin's Head* (detail)
25 11/16" X 58"   MHS # 1931.850

❧ *Acknowledgments* ❧

FIRST, WE THANK THE CHAMPIONS who encouraged this work across a span of more than 50 years.

In 1961 Francis H. Lloyd, Executive Secretary of the Marblehead Historical Society (MHS), welcomed Priscilla and provided unprecedented access to the archives and paintings that inspired this story. The Board of Directors of the MHS generously granted permission to conduct the research and take photographs that were fundamental to the project.

During more recent years, Pam Peterson, Director of the Marblehead Museum and Historical Society (MMHS), not only urged us to create this book, but also converted her expertise into a Foreword that brings Marblehead history to its readers. Karen Mac Innis, the Curator of MMHS, joined our team to provide access to the archives, confirm historical and bibliographic accuracy, and provide the digital files that were essential to reproduce the art of J.O.J. Frost. Our deepest appreciation goes to both Pam and Karen for their time, enthusiasm, and good humor when this project was added to their very busy schedules.

We also want to acknowledge the Cape Ann Museum in Gloucester, Massachusetts, and the Peabody Essex Museum (PEM) in Salem, Massachusetts, for the exhibits and ship models that aided the visualization of the story. Special thanks go to Daniel Finamore, Curator of Maritime Art and History at the PEM, for confirming several hypotheses inherent to the story.

We want to thank Nancy Lee Swift for her eagle eyes and professional critiques that strengthened the manuscript and helped us avoid a few shoals.

For her outstanding editing, book production, and wise counsel, we thank Brookes Nohlgren of Books by Brookes. For her creative design and problem-solving, we thank Peri Poloni-Gabriel of Knockout Design.

Loving appreciation goes to Bruce W. Moulton; without his seamanship and nautical expertise, *Molly Waldo!* would certainly have gone aground. Furthermore, his artistic sensibility provided a "true north" throughout this journey.

And, finally, we thank our husbands for their companionship and patience during this long voyage.

❧ About the Authors ❧

PRISCILLA L. MOULTON championed the authors and illustrators of children's books throughout her professional career: developing school libraries, organizing events to promote children's books, reviewing for the *Horn Book Magazine*, and publishing *Phaedrus* (an international journal on children's literature). In leadership positions in the American Library Association, Priscilla participated in selecting several Newbery and Caldecott Medal winners.

In 1959, as a new resident of Marblehead, Massachusetts, Priscilla first saw the paintings of J.O.J. Frost hanging in the historical society's Lee Mansion. Struck by their storytelling power, she began to envision a book about Marblehead's history as a fishing community. Her research for that purpose became the foundation for *Molly Waldo!* This book for all ages pays tribute to an American historian and artist, as well as to the place that became home for the Moulton family.

BETHE LEE MOULTON shares her mother's love for Marblehead. Learning to sail in the harbor, taking piano lessons next to General Glover's home and visiting Old Burial Hill are a few of the experiences that shaped the author of *Molly Waldo!*

Bethe left Marblehead to attend Cornell University, Case Western Reserve University and the Harvard Business School. As an international strategist, she worked in 30 countries on five continents and became interested in the concept of journey as a source of self-discovery. Her first novel, *Until Brazil*, and *Molly Waldo!*, a work of historical fiction, both explore the theme — "Journeys Afar for Discoveries Within."

After an international career, Bethe founded The Glide Press as one means to reconnect with books and boats — two interests instilled by her mother and father. The *Glide* is a graceful black yawl that was once a familiar sight in Marblehead Harbor. Sailing aboard the *Glide*, Bethe developed a deep respect for the sea and the skippers who make it home. In that spirit, she offers *Molly Waldo!* to its readers.

The GLIDE *Press*

www.theglidepress.com